STEPHANIE
ROWE

Dark Wolf
UNBOUND

DARK WOLF UNBOUND (*Heart of the Shifter #2)*
Copyright © 2016 by Stephanie Rowe
Cover design © 2015 by Kelli Ann Morgan,
www.inspirecreativeservices.com

ISBN-10: 1-940968-26-7
ISBN-13: 978-1-940968-26-1

For further information, please contact:
Stephanie@stephanierowe.com

Dedication

For AR, who makes every moment a little brighter.

Acknowledgements

Special thanks to my beta readers and the Rockstars. You guys are the best! There are so many to thank by name, more than I could count, but here are those who I want to called out specially for all they did to help this book come to life: Malinda Davis Diehl, Leslie Barnes, Kayla Bartley, Alencia Bates Salters, Alyssa Bird, Donna Bossert, Jean Bowden, Shell Bryce, Kelley Daley Curry, Ashley Cuesta, Denise Fluhr, Sandi Foss, Valerie Glass, Heidi Hoffman, Jeanne Stone, Rebecca Johnson, Dottie Jones, Janet Juengling-Snell, Deb Julienne, Bridget Koan, Felicia Low, Phyllis Marshall, Suzanne Mayer, Jodi Moore, Ashlee Murphy, Elizabeth Neal, Judi Pflughoeft, Carol Pretorius, Kasey Richardson, Caryn Santee, Amber Ellison Shriver, Summer Steelman, Regina Thomas, and Linda Watson. Special thanks to my family, who I love with every fiber of my heart and soul. And to AER, who is my world. Love you so much, baby girl!

Dark Wolf
UNBOUND

Chapter One

JACE DONOVAN DIDN'T hesitate.

The moment his SUV pulled up in front of the old ranch house buried in the woods on the banks of the Hood Canal in Washington, Jace kicked open the door and stepped out onto the damp ground. The winter rains had created a muddy mess, but it mattered little to him. Nothing mattered to him right now. The pain from his shattered ankle was excruciating, but he kept his weight evenly distributed on both feet, out of habit. No wolf shifter showed weakness and lived long enough to regret it.

His two pack mates, Cash Burns and Drake London, got out of the vehicle and walked up so they were flanking him, both of them close enough to grab him if all hell broke loose.

Jace grimly studied the decrepit house. The paint was peeling, the shutters were broken, and the lawn was an overgrown swamp of moss, mud, and weeds. His black mood became even darker at the sight of the squalor. The Stevens family had so little, and yet he'd still managed to find something to steal from them. Not just *something*. He'd stolen the only thing that mattered.

"You have the guns?" he asked his escorts, keeping his gaze on the run-down house.

"We're not going to shoot you," Cash said evenly.

"Do you have the guns?" he asked again, making it clear that he wasn't going to even acknowledge that mutinous statement.

"Shit, Jace, you're not going to lose control and murder them," Drake said. "Grigori is gone. He doesn't control you anymore."

Jace said nothing. He just stood there, watching the house, waiting. He wasn't going to explain it again. It was their job to do as he instructed, and if he showed weakness, he knew they would never do it. Yeah, he was their alpha, but he was more than that. These two men were his deepest friends and his greatest allies. If Jace gave them any leeway at all, he knew they would never put a bullet into him when the moment came.

So, he waited, not looking at them, not lowering himself to respond. He used the blistering pain in his ankle to distract himself, adjusting his stance to put even more weight on the ankle that had been crushed in a recent fight with the psychopath Grigori and Jace's deputy, Damien, who Grigori had co-opted.

Finally, Cash and Drake exchanged glances, and Cash shrugged. "Fine, yeah, we have the guns. If you go after anyone, we'll stop you."

Tension wrapped tighter around Jace's spine. "No matter what it takes."

Cash sighed. "No matter what it takes."

Satisfaction pulsed through Jace. He wasn't going to pretend he was happy to die. The last thing he fucking wanted was to get a silver bullet between his eyes, but he wasn't going to let one more innocent die by his hands. If killing him was necessary to protect others, then killing him was what needed to happen.

"Then we go in." He strode forward without hesitation, heading right for the front door. With each step on his injured leg, his body shook in agony, but he welcomed the pain. Each shard of pain was a reminder of what he'd done, for letting his wolf control him. He deserved a shattered ankle, and a part of him was still pissed that the doctors had worked so hard to save it.

As Jace neared the house, Cash and Drake stayed so close that their trench coats brushed his legs. He hadn't gone anywhere without Cash and Drake since he'd been released from prison. They were his body-guards now, but their job wasn't to protect him. It was to protect others from him. He knew he was a ticking time bomb, but he didn't know what trigger would make him finally explode.

He slammed his fist on the door and then stepped back.

Waiting.

There was no sound from inside.

Swearing under his breath, he hit the door with his fist again. "Hello!" he shouted. "Is anyone home?"

This time, he heard the faint shuffle of footsteps inside. Tension shot through him, and he jumped back, moving slightly behind Cash and Drake. Sweat broke out over his palms as the footsteps neared the front door. Someone was walking toward the door, toward him. Someone who once could have trusted him, could now become his victim in a split second.

The song, that fucking song, began to play in his head again, and he swore, slamming his fists to his forehead. *Shut the fuck up.* Sweat trickled down his back as he fought to silence that song, but he could still hear it, faintly, drifting through the edges of his mind.

Ever since he'd heard that song and it had forced him to shift and murder, the song had continued to haunt him, drifting through his mind on its own, as if it were a wraith that was slithering through his mind, waiting for the right time to incite him to attack.

He knew he should leave. He shouldn't be here. But he owed this family, and he trusted Cash and Drake to shut him down. "Knife," he commanded Cash. "Get the knife ready." The song was getting louder in his head. How loud did it have to get before it forced him to shift, before it turned him into a murderer again? He'd been able to resist the song ever since that night, but it was stronger right now than it had ever been, crawling through his veins like an insidious poison.

Cash glanced over at him. His eyes widened at whatever expression he saw on Jace's face, and he immediately reached into his coat pocket. Jace knew that his fingers were now wrapped around the handle of a silver-bladed knife, ready to strike.

The knife wouldn't kill him, but the hit of silver in his veins would hurt him enough for Drake to shoot him.

The door handle began to turn, and the song played even louder in his head. Swearing, Jace dug into his own pocket and wrapped his fingers around the silk bag containing two silver balls. He dumped the contents into his palm, and his skin began to burn the moment the silver touched his hand. He gritted his jaw against the pain, summoning all his discipline to keep himself from jerking his hand out of his pocket and away from the silver.

The pain in his hand was so consuming that he was barely able to focus when the door opened, revealing a gray-haired woman in a pair of black pants and a red cardigan. Her eyes were bright blue, sparkling with more life than he would have expected, given her stooped shoulders and the trauma he'd put her through.

He cleared his throat and pulled his shoulders back, keeping his fist tight around the silver balls and leaning more of his weight onto his broken ankle. The pain was excruciating, but it worked, leaving no room in his mind for songs. "Mrs. Stevens?" he asked.

The woman's silver-white eyebrows went up. "I'm Nancy Collins. No Stevens here." Her eyes were bright, but there was an edge to her voice that spoke of a heavy weight in her soul.

"None?" Had he gotten the wrong house?

No, he was certain of his information. This was the last registered home address of Melissa. He quickly concluded that this must be the grandmother. No one from her family had come to the trial, so he had no way to recognize anyone. "Are you the mother or grandmother of Melissa Stevens?" His voice caught as he said the name of the woman he'd murdered. Jesus.

Pain flickered across the woman's face. "Not mother. Grandmother," she said softly. "My poor girls. First Jessica, and then her daughter, dying the same way."

The same way? The mother had been murdered too? *Jesus.* What the fuck had he brought upon this woman? The gaping emptiness that had been haunting him since that night expanded, sucking him down. He knew this was it. He was done after this. As an alpha, there had been instances where he'd had to make the choice to end the life of another shifter, after he'd concluded that it was an irredeemable threat to society. He never took the task lightly, but protecting innocents was the very foundation of who he was. The song had turned him into the same monster that he'd had to destroy, and now, it was his turn.

There was just one last thing to do before he took the fate he deserved.

Slowly, he went down on his knees and bowed his head. "My name is Jace Donovan," he said. "I—"

"Jace Donovan?" The woman sucked in her breath, apparently recognizing his name. "You bastard!"

He didn't lift his head, staring at the weeds growing out of the cracked cement on the stoop. "I know. I know there is no forgiveness for what I did. I know nothing I can do will bring her back. But I owe you and your family an apology. I am sorry, on every level of my soul, for killing your granddaughter. I—"

"You think it's an excuse that someone else was controlling you?" she hissed. "You think that makes it okay?"

He looked up, what was left of his soul crumbling when he saw the tears shining on her cheeks. "No," he said. "I don't think it makes it okay. That's why I'm here to apologize." He suddenly had an idea, and he looked over at Cash. "Give her the gun."

"What?" Cash looked shocked. "No."

"Give her the gun." As the pack alpha, Jace knew that Cash had no choice but to follow his orders. He looked at Nancy. "I give you the honor of killing me."

Her eyes widened. "What are you talking about? I don't want to shoot you."

"You deserve the closure." He glared at Cash. "Give her the gun."

Cash shook his head. "No!"

"It has to be done. I was going to do it, but it's better this way." He turned toward the woman, whose eyes had gone wide as she watched the exchange. "Killing your granddaughter violated every moral code I have," he said. "I agree that it is irrelevant that Grigori was controlling me. That's no excuse. Any wolf shifter that's a threat to the safety of innocents must die, and I'm no exception. I give you the honor."

"Fuck that." Cash glared at him. "You're not going to kill yourself because some piece of shit manipulated you. We need you."

Jace lurched to his feet, scowling back at Cash. "Do you realize I hear that fucking song in my head all the time? That I can feel my body wanting to shift? He doesn't even have to be near me to trigger it. Whatever he did to me is still in there, and it's just a matter of time until it wins again. Then what? Should I make a pilgrimage to apologize again to the next family? And then the next? Fuck that, Cash! I'm a liability, and I can't be allowed to live. It's your turn to take over the pack, so back the fuck off and give her the damn gun!"

The front door slammed shut, jerking Jace's attention back to the door. Nancy was gone, and he heard the lock on the front door click. "Shit!" He rapped his knuckles on the door again. "I'm sorry. I didn't mean to scare you. I—"

"Stop." Drake put his hand on Jace's shoulder. "It's over. She absolved you by refusing to kill you."

Jace bowed his head, leaning his forehead against the worn-out front door, anguish consuming him. "I scared her," he whispered. "I came here to apologize, and I made it worse." Darkness pressed down on him, and he closed his eyes, unwilling to summon the strength to fight it off anymore. The guilt that had been crushing him so mercilessly since that night surged around him, tearing apart what little was left of his soul. He decided to let the song take him, to surrender to it and to make the decision easy for Cash and Drake.

He dropped to his knees and grabbed the door-frame, leaning his head against the wood. "Do it."

Cash tensed. "Fuck no. Get up."

Jace knew then that they didn't believe him. They had no concept of the power of the song that was still in his head. They had no understanding of how deadly it could turn him in a split second, a monster utterly devoid of any kind of mercy or humanity.

He closed his eyes, and, for the first time since the murder, he intentionally attuned his mind to the song. He listened to it, breathing in each note, each word, each waft of power. It began to build inside him, and heat began to rise off his body.

"Son of a bitch," Drake said. "He's calling the song. He's trying to force us to kill him."

"Jace!" Cash commanded. "Look at me!"

Jace kept his head down, and continued to listen to the song. His skin began to prickle.

"Throw the gun away," Cash shouted at Drake. "Get rid of it!"

"But if he shifts—"

"Ditch it!"

Jace heard the thud of a gun hitting the ground a hundred yards away, and he swore. "Don't!" He looked up just as Drake threw his gun into the woods. "You idiots!" He lurched to his feet. "What the fuck are you doing?"

"Saving your life!" Cash grabbed him by the shirt and threw him up against the door. "You're our alpha! If you shift now and murder us, then you violate your oath to protect your pack. Pull it together, Jace! Do it now or you're going to kill us!"

The song was louder now, almost at full strength. Jace swore and jammed his hand into his pocket, grabbing the silver balls. Pain knifed through him, but the song continued to scream through his mind. He couldn't shift right now. There was no one to stop him, and there was a little old lady behind a decrepit door, and his two pack mates, all of whom would be targets for his insanity. Shit! He had to resist the song, but it was too strong now, taking over him with ruthless efficiency. "The knife," he commanded. "Get it!"

Cash pulled the knife out and sliced Jace's shirt open. He pressed the flat of the silver blade across Jace's chest, right over his heart.

"Son of a bitch," Jace gasped as smoke began to rise from his skin. His heart stuttered, and lurched, and he collapsed to his knees. Drake caught him as he went down, holding him up enough so Cash didn't lose contact with the knife. He began to cough, trying to suck air into his lungs, as his body fought to defend itself against the silver. All his energy surged toward his heart, focused only on survival, stealing energy from the song.

"You got it now?" Cash asked, his face grim.

Jace nodded, gripping his chest as Cash removed the blade. He swore, his heart pounding erratically. His lungs didn't seem to work, and he jerked his hand out of his pocket, releasing the silver balls. His body was struggling in response to all the silver, fighting to regain equilibrium.

"Let's get him to the woods." Drake grabbed one arm, and Cash the other.

Jace stumbled, trying to regain his feet while the

others helped him toward the trees. The moment he reached the edge of the forest, they eased him down to the ground. He collapsed, his face pressed against the wet earth. He concentrated on the richness of the soil, drawing the energy of the earth into his damaged body. Slowly, his heartbeat steadied, and he was able to take a deep breath.

He rolled onto his back, staring up at the faces of his two most trusted pack mates. Neither of them looked even mildly apologetic for openly disobeying their alpha. "You guys suck."

They both grinned unrepentantly. "Sometimes the best follower is the one who knows when to ignore orders," Cash said.

"And what about when I finally snap and kill someone else?" Jace asked.

Drake shrugged, his broad shoulders lifting his heavy jacket. "I got no life. I'm fine with following you around every second of the day. We could have a bromance."

Cash coughed and turned away, covering his mouth with his arm, doing a shoddy job covering his amusement.

Jace scowled at Drake "A bromance? Really? That's your solution?"

Drake's smile faded and he crouched beside Jace. "You saved our asses when we were lost," he said, his voice low and urgent. "Cash and I would both be dead with a trail of victims behind us if you hadn't saved us. We weren't innocent, but you fought for us because you believed in us. There's no fucking chance we're abandoning you, no matter what, so give it up. You might not have a pristine resume anymore, but that's not what life is about. Stains make you greater than you already were, and we're not letting you knock yourself off because some bastard worked you over."

Jace glanced at Cash, who nodded his agreement. "What he said."

Something inside Jace turned over. He was proud of how these men had turned out. They weren't that much younger than he was, and he knew they were the brothers he'd never had. He treasured their loyalty and belief more than he could ever say, but he also knew their faith was misplaced.

He was not the hero they wanted him to be; however, they deserved more than to be burdened with killing him.

He wouldn't ask that of them.

He would take that responsibility upon himself, when they weren't around.

Someday, they would understand.

Chapter Two

ABBY Collins watched through a crack in the yellowed curtains, watching the three shifters. Jace was down on the ground, and the other two were standing guard, clearly protecting him. "I can feel his pain, Nana," she said softly.

Her grandmother dug her bony fingers into Abby's elbow, peering over her shoulder to watch Jace. "He's alpha. Like Grigori."

"I know," Abby said, well aware of the implications of that truth.

Jace sat up slowly, his face drawn and peaked, his eyes haunted with deep anguish and self-hate. His leather bomber jacket and jeans were caked in mud, but he didn't appear to care. He just rested his forearms on his knees, staring moodily at the house.

Her skin prickled at the intensity of his stare, even though she knew he couldn't see her through the lacy curtains. He was broken, but at the same time, power rolled off him in thick waves. It was the strength of the wolf, but also something more, something deeper,

something that came from within and thundered out-
ward into all that surrounded him. Awareness rippled
through her, not just of him as a threat, but as a man.
"He's dangerous."

"He's a murderer." Nana spit on the floor and made
the sign of the cross on her chest.

Tears burned in Abby's eyes at the reminder of
what she'd lost, but she pushed them aside, refusing to
be sucked into the debilitating grief of her sister's
death. She had to stay focused. There was too much at
stake. She couldn't afford to crumble in a pool of emotions right now. "I know he is." But she'd also been at
the trial, hiding from the press behind sunglasses and a
hat. She'd heard his defense. She'd seen his torment.
She'd listened to his pack mates defend his honor with
such passion that she knew they were speaking from
the heart.

No truly evil man could summon such deep, untainted support unless there was something redeemable
about him. Jace was a murderer, yes, but it was more
complicated than that, so much more complicated.

"He's a demon," Nana hissed. "He murdered your
sister. He walks on four legs, and comes to life under
the full moon. He's an animal, a creature destined for
damnation since the day he was born, just like all shifters."

"Not all shifters are evil." But even as she said it,
fear rippled down Abby's spine, and she turned her
head to look out the window again. She'd lived among
shifters for most of her life. She knew how deadly they
could be. She'd lived among evil. She'd done her share
of it. But she'd also seen shifters who loved, protected,
and treasured their loved ones…

She swallowed, closing her eyes against the memories she worked so hard to suppress. *Not now, Abby. Not now.* She took a deep breath, then opened her eyes to study Jace. She slipped her fingers between the curtain panels and parted them just enough so she had an unobstructed view of him. He was a killer, and all that separated her from him was a pane of glass that could be shattered easily with one strike of his fist.

"You need his help," Nana said grimly, moving beside her to gaze out the window. She didn't bother to part the curtain. She just stared through the yellowed, loosely woven fabric, as if she wanted to keep that barrier between them.

"What?" Abby looked sharply at her grandmother, unable to stop the surge of anticipation at the idea of reaching out to him. Something about Jace called to her. It had ever since she'd seen him limp into the courtroom, his shoulders slumped, his eyes so lost. "Help for what?"

"Ask him to help you find Seth. It's the only way."

"Ask *him?*" Abby bit her lip, studying Jace's anguished face. His beard looked like an untamed mess of whiskers he hadn't shaved in days. His shoulders were hunched. He looked like a man who'd been destroyed, not a powerful alpha who had done the unthinkable for his pack, again and again, if the rumors were to be believed. Yet, at the same time, his body rippled with muscle, and his jaw was hard. He was elemental power, dragged down by the guilt she knew so well. "He killed Melissa," she said quietly, testing the truth aloud. "He ripped out her throat." She bit back tears, trying not to replay the horror of that night.

Nana looked at her, her wise eyes narrowed. "You know how powerful Grigori is. It takes a shifter of comparable power to stop him. Jace is that wolf. *You must stop Grigori."*

"I just..." She tightened her fingers on the curtain as Jace stood up. He staggered slightly, and she saw his face tighten in pain as he shifted to put more of his weight onto his injured leg. He began to walk back toward the house, staring at the window she was standing in, as if he could see her through the brittle curtain.

Her heart began to pound as he got closer and she could see him more clearly. Although he was clearly in pain, he moved like a predator, smoothly, stealthily, his muscles rippling with power. She'd heard the anguish in his voice through the front door, when he'd been talking to her grandmother, and then to his friends, trying to get them to shoot him, but to see it in his eyes as he got closer was heartbreaking. Tears burned in her own eyes, both for his pain, and for her own. So much loss.

He walked right up to the window and grabbed the frame, his eyes boring into hers.

She froze, suddenly realizing that he was looking right at her. Somehow, he'd known she was there, even when he'd been sitting in the woods. He was bigger than she'd expected, his shoulders nearly as wide as the window.

She started to step back, but Nana pushed her forward in a swift, rough shove. Abby crashed into the window, her hands smacking against the glass. The curtain had parted, giving her a clear view of the man who'd murdered her sister.

His dark eyes were haunted and empty. His jaw was flexed. His short dark hair was shiny with the rain, rivulets sliding down his face. "I'm sorry," he said, his voice easily audible through the glass. "I'm so fucking sorry."

Her heart turned over at the grief in his voice. He was soaking wet, dripping with mud and rain, yet he didn't move. He just stood there, on the other side of the glass, searching her face, waiting for something from her. Forgiveness? No, she didn't think he wanted that. Peace?

Yes, that was it. He wanted to give her peace.

She flattened her hand against the glass, as if she could reach through it. He hesitated for a split second, and then he set his hand against the pane, pressing his palm to hers, with only the thin glass between them.

The heat from his palm surged through the glass, making it feel as though she was touching his skin. Awareness prickled through her, an awareness that came from deep in her belly and surged through her. She leaned forward, instinctively closing the distance between them, *needing* to be closer to him.

Behind her, her grandmother swore, and then she reached past Abby and touched the glass where Jace's hand was. "Son of a bitch," her grandmother muttered. "He's not like the others. He's different. That piece of shit Grigori broke him. He's the one, Abby. You need him. He needs you." Her gnarled fingers curled into a fist as she pulled back. "He's the one who can end it," she whispered.

"What? He can't help me," Abby whispered, watching as he raised his other hand and placed it on the glass. She mimicked his move, placing her other hand so it was directly aligned with his, so both their hands were pressed against each other. "He's too broken. And he's a murderer. You said it yourself." But even as she said it, she moved closer to the window, to him, to the sheer power he generated. She felt like a moth drawn to a bright light that could either burn her up, or give her the warmth she needed to survive.

"He is a murderer, but he is also more. I can feel it pouring from him. I know you do as well."

"Is he?" Abby searched the face of the man before her. The rain was hammering against the glass, creating streaks that made it more difficult to see him. Her own breath was beginning to fog up the glass, obscuring her view of him. She wiped the fog away, her palm squeaking against the cold glass.

He met her gaze, and her heart seemed to shatter at the depth of pain in his eyes. She knew that pain, because she lived with it every day. "Jace," she whispered, her fingers curving against the glass, as if she could entangle her fingers with his, as if she could somehow relieve both their pain by connecting physically with him. But it was only glass beneath her hand, not his skin. She closed her eyes, unable to bear the memories that he brought back to her.

"He's leaving," Nana said, her gnarled fingers digging into Abby's arm. "Don't let him go. Without him, you can't fulfill your promise to Melissa to find her son. Seth will be lost forever, if you don't get this man to help you. You know what Grigori will do to Seth if you don't find him first. Melissa died trying to protect her son, and it's up to you now. He's your nephew, your godson, and he's counting on you."

Abby opened her eyes, and with a twist of regret and an inexplicable sense of loss, she saw that Jace had turned away. He was walking back to his car, flanked by his two pack mates, the men who'd testified on his behalf at the murder trial, gaining him exoneration. He'd murdered her sister. *He'd murdered her sister.* Her grandmother despised him…but at the same time, she was calling him Abby's only hope.

How could she go to him? How could she work with him? How could she trust him? *How could she trust herself around him*? She was the reason he was suffering. She was the one who'd broken him. She was the one he should despise. She was the one who represented the greatest risk to him.

They were each other's greatest nightmare...and yet, at the same time, her soul called out to him. Her body craved his touch. Her heart needed resolution with him. And, on a purely mercenary level, she needed his help. How could she turn down her one chance to save her nephew from the monster who'd had both his father and mother murdered?

She couldn't.

* * *

Jace's fingers had just closed around the cold door handle of his SUV when he heard the front door open. He froze, not turning around, every sense attuned behind him.

"Jace! Wait!"

The command rang out in the rain, wrapping around him like a compulsion. Her voice was beautiful, feminine, and strong, plunging right past his walls deep into his gut. He knew it belonged to the woman he'd glimpsed behind the curtain, whose face he'd barely been able to discern through the rain-splattered glass and heavy lace drapery. He'd been able to make out the slant of her nose, the angle of her jaw, and the curve of her neck. Her hands, though, he knew. He'd felt her palms, pressed up against the glass against his. Her hands had been small and delicate, but pulsing with an inner strength that had drawn him.

And now, he could hear her footsteps splashing through the mud as she ran toward him.

He turned instinctively, years of habit as an alpha propelling him to face her so she couldn't approach from behind. His gut turned over when he saw her running toward him. She was wearing jeans and a gray sweatshirt, her bare feet sinking into the mud up to her ankles as she ran. Her hips were curved, her legs long and decadent, her feet slim and vulnerable in the mud. Her hair was light brown, tumbling around her shoulders, already getting wet in the rain. She had all the curves of a woman, but she was small and delicate, calling out his protective instincts. His body responded instantly, shockingly, to her femininity and her vulnerability, need pulsing through him to claim her right then.

Anticipation built inside him as she neared, but it was when she was close enough to see her eyes that he became utterly riveted. They were deep green, almost the color of an emerald, so starkly beautiful and bright it felt surreal in the wet, gray woods they were standing in. She slipped as she neared him, and he instinctively leapt forward and caught her before she could fall, his fingers closing around her upper arms.

She grabbed his forearms for balance, staring at him in surprise. For a split second, the world seemed to vanish, and all that remained was her, them, this moment. The sensation of having his fingers wrapped around her arms was shocking in its intensity. Every nerve in his body was taut, suspended in anticipation of her next move, her next words, her next request. She was surreal temptation, calling to his wolf on a level no female had ever summoned before. He wanted her. He wanted to drag her into his arms, kiss her, claim her, and make her his.

Her eyes widened, and she caught her breath.

He could hear her pulse thundering, as if she'd been thrust into the same frenzy of attraction that had caught him. His fingers tightened as hunger roared through him, obliterating everything but *her.* She didn't pull away, and his gaze went to her mouth. Her lips were pale pink, bare, and tempting. The need to kiss her howled through him, and for a split second, he could think of nothing else to do but claim her mouth with his—

Her cheeks turned red, and she pulled back.

He released her instantly, shoving his hands into his pockets to keep from reaching for her. *Shit.* What had that been about? He wasn't here to seduce. He was here to find a way to abate the damage from what he'd done.

But she didn't give him the chance to retreat. She stuck out her hand as if to shake his. "My name is Abby Collins. Melissa was my sister."

Melissa's *sister?* She was the *sister* of the woman he'd murdered? His stomach turned, and he took her hand. Shaking it felt stupid and superficial, so he pressed her cold hand between both of his, trying to will warmth into it. "I'm so fucking sorry," he said. It felt easier to say it this time, as if the words were finally becoming a part of him.

"I know." She searched his face, as if she were looking for secrets he never shared with anyone. "I need your help."

"My help? Of course." He nodded immediately, still not releasing her hand. Why wasn't she looking at him in fear? Why wasn't she shuddering at the touch of his flesh? He knew he should let go of her hand, but it felt so fucking incredible to be holding it. It was easier to breathe when he was touching her, as if she was pouring life back into him simply through her touch "What can I do?"

Her gaze flicked to Drake and Cash, who were still standing right beside him. "Can we talk alone for a moment?"

"No." He didn't hesitate. "They're here for your safety. We talk here."

"I—" She grimaced. "Please?"

For a split second, he almost considered it. He owed her so much. If she wanted privacy, then she deserved it. But at the same time, he couldn't put her at risk. "No."

She studied his face. "You're afraid the song will make you shift, aren't you? Like it did when you killed my sister. You still hear it in your head, don't you?"

He stared at her, so shocked by her insight that he didn't have an answer. How did she know?

"Do you hear it now?" she asked.

He realized suddenly that he didn't. His subconscious was quiet, his entire being focused completely on her. The silver had worked to decrease the song's grip on his mind, but Abby had wiped it away completely. "No."

She smiled, a breathtakingly warm smile that made him want to drop to his knees and ask her to smile forever, just for him, just to make him realize that the world wasn't always shrouded in darkness. "Then we're good." She tugged at his hand, and began to back up. "Come on," she said, her voice taut with urgency. "Please?"

He wanted to go with her. He wanted to give her whatever she asked for, not just because he owed her for taking away her sister, but because she made him feel like he could breathe for the first time in a very long time. It was selfish, but he couldn't help it. He was simply so desperate to feel human again, and somehow, she gave him hope that it was possible.

"Go," Cash said. "I'll retrieve the gun. I can take you out from a distance, as long as you're within shooting range." As he spoke, Drake turned away and jogged toward the woods where they'd tossed the guns. Within a moment, he'd found one of them, and he held it up, making a silent promise to use it.

Jace took a deep breath, but he knew that he owed Abby so much for stealing her sister. He could give her privacy, if that was what she wanted. He trusted Drake and Cash with the guns. They were great marksmen. He hoped that she was going to berate him, to unleash her anguish and fury out on him. "Okay."

Fear gnawing at him that he would turn on her, he allowed her to lead the way to the side of the house, her feet sinking into the mud. "You need shoes," he said.

What an inane comment. Shoes? What the fuck was he obsessing about shoes for? He was there to apologize for murdering her sister for hell's sake. He had no right to feel protective of her, to want to protect her feet from the cold mud.

"I prefer barefoot," she said. She pulled him next to the house and turned to face him. Tension radiated off her, and then he saw fear in her eyes, the fear he'd been expecting from the outset. The fear was appropriate, but it also bit deep, eating away at him.

He gritted his jaw, disgusted that he'd become something that people feared. He'd been so arrogant his whole life, thinking he controlled the wolf that paced inside him, and it had all been a delusion. Scowling, he checked to make sure that Cash and

Drake still had a clear shot at him. They did, and he was satisfied to see that they were both watching him carefully, the guns held loosely in their right hands.

Reassured that he would be dead before he could hurt her, he turned his attention to Abby again. "How can I help you?" he asked again. He knew there was nothing he could do that would change what had happened, but he'd cut out his own heart and hand it to her if she asked, if it would help her.

She bit her lower lip for a second, as if she had to take a moment to hold back her emotions. "My sister had a son."

"Fuck." He turned away and ran his hand through his hair. It just kept getting worse. Melissa had a kid. "What about his dad?"

She flinched. "He's dead. He wasn't a good man. It was just the two of them."

Jace closed his eyes against the swell of grief. He'd orphaned a child? He'd fucking *orphaned* a child? For a moment, he couldn't breathe. His lungs seemed to close down on him, sucking the life from him. Swearing, he fought for control. He couldn't succumb to the vacuum threatening to consume him. Dying would be the easy way out. He had to stand here. He had to face it. He had to fix it. He gritted his jaw and turned back toward Abby, refusing to allow himself to hide from her. "He'll need money. I'll set up a fund for him. He'll be set for life financially. I—"

She held up her hand to silence him, and he immediately stopped, cold fingers of dread clamping around his spine. She wasn't finished. It got worse. "What?" he asked, his voice hoarse. "What else?"

"Grigori kidnapped him."

Horror sucker-punched Jace in the gut. "Grigori

took the boy?" A cold sweat broke out on his palms. Grigori was a psychotic, serial killer who had forced his entire pack to kill on command. He was a ruthless, deadly psychopath with no remorse or value for life. He was the one who'd invented a song that could force a shifter into wolf form and turn him into a merciless killer. "How?"

"Seth was in the apartment with my sister, and when she went out the fire escape to run from you, Grigori came in the front door and kidnapped him."

"Jesus." His legs gave out and he sank to his knees, unable to hold himself up.

"Jace." Abby knelt in front of him, putting her hand on his shoulder. "He used you to get her out of the way so he could take Seth. It was always about Seth, not you or Melissa." She hesitated, then offered a platitude that he knew she didn't believe. "It's not your fault."

"Not my fault? Fuck that. *Fuck that.*" Her sympathy pissed him off. No one should be feeling sorry for him. He should be held accountable for what he'd done. No alpha should have been susceptible to being forced to shift and kill a woman. He was completely responsible for his actions. "Why did he want the child?" Anger surged through Jace, and fear, a deep-seated *terror* for that child. Gone was the anguish and depression, replaced by a fierce, desperate protective-ness toward the boy he didn't even know. But he knew what Grigori was capable of, and the thought of an innocent child in Grigori's claws was horrifying.

Her lips tightened, and he knew she wasn't going to answer him. She was hiding something.

"Did you get him back yet?" he asked, but he already knew the answer.

"No." She met his gaze. "They've vanished. I've

talked to some private investigators. They either can't find him, or they refused to take the case. Everyone is afraid of Grigori. I need your help, Jace. You're my only chance."

He surged to his feet, pacing away from her, his mind spinning as he raced through the possibilities. "What can I do?" He'd searched for Grigori too, but he hadn't found a trace. None of them had. The shifter had vanished completely, along with his pack.

Desperation flickered across her face. "Maybe you can track Seth. If we go back to my sister's apartment, you might be able to connect with him. Grigori can hide his presence easily, but Seth is too young. You're a powerful shifter, Jace. If anyone can track him, you can." She grabbed his arm, her fingers so small and delicate around his wrist. "Can you track him, Jace? Can you find him before it's too late?"

Jace knew Grigori would force the boy to kill innocents. If a wolf acquired a taste for hunting before he learned to control the wolf, it would turn him into a monster that could never be saved.... Son of a bitch. Was that what this was about? He looked at Abby. "Is Seth a shifter? Is that why Grigori wanted him? To turn him into another one of his deadly soldiers?"

For a long moment, Abby didn't respond. Then she nodded. "Yes."

He could see in her eyes that she wasn't telling him the entire truth, but it was enough. The boy was one of Jace's kind, and that meant he was under his protection. The fact that he owed the kid's family a debt he could never repay was an added incentive. He would save that damn kid, no matter what the cost to himself. "I'll find him and bring him here when I locate him."

He started to turn away, but she grabbed his arm.

"Jace."

He looked over at her. "What?"

"I'm going with you."

He went cold, ice cold, as his reality came slamming back at him. He grabbed her shoulders and pushed her back against the house, trapping her against the wet wood. "Don't you get it, Abby? I fucking murdered your sister. Grigori took that song and he turned me into a monster. It's still in my head, and at *any second*, I could lose the battle and kill you. There's no fucking chance that I'm going to take the risk of turning on you. You don't get to come."

She lifted her chin. "You need me."

"Why?"

She hesitated, then answered, her gaze flicking away from his for a split second before she answered. "I know Grigori better than you do. If you find him, I can help."

Her words stopped him. He studied her more carefully. She looked unsophisticated and outdoorsy in her jeans and sweatshirt. She looked like a woman who wouldn't mind hanging out with wolves, but at the same time, there was a fragility to her that would have made her a target among a group of predators. "How do you know him?"

She looked away again. "It doesn't matter—"

"Fuck that." He clasped her jaw and turned her head so she was looking at him. He chose his words carefully. "Grigori is a psychopath. He uses mind control to force wolves to shift and murder. He cares about nothing other than power and carnage. He would kill his own children if it benefitted him. Going after him is a doomed mission unless I do it right. So, tell me what you know. *How do you know him?*"

27

He felt her summon her strength, and then she looked right at him, her gaze steady. "Because I'm his daughter."

Chapter Three

Jace's Entire Body went cold, and he jerked his hands back from her, as if she'd burned him. "You're his *daughter*?" Grigori was the psychopath who had twisted Jace's mind until he'd murdered an innocent woman. He was a predator who had left scores of victims in his wake across several continents. A beast so vile that he contaminated everyone he touched. How could he possibly be the father of this woman standing before him?

But Abby nodded in affirmation, her eyes watching him warily. "Yes."

Jesus. His mind raced, trying to put all the pieces together into a model that made sense. "Was Melissa his daughter, too? And your mom? His…mate?"

At her nod, he swore under his breath. What kind of situation had he walked into? "If Melissa was his daughter, why did he have me kill her?" He knew Grigori was vile, but what monster orchestrated the brutal murder of his own child? Jace couldn't even fathom that. His instinct to protect ran so deeply through him that he would give his life to save anyone in his circle, and his own child would be even more precious than that.

"My mom met him when she was fifteen," Abby explained. "She was young and in a tough situation. She was incredibly beautiful, however, and he decided he wanted her. He offered her sanctuary and attention, overwhelming her with all the things she wanted and needed. He never let her see what he really was, until she was so under his spell that she was blind to his depravity."

The pain that flashed across her face made pain twist through his gut. "You grew up in his pack?" At her nod, anger tore through him, a dark, possessive fury. "What did he do to you?"

She lifted her chin defiantly, and he saw the flash of anger in her eyes, a refusal to submit to the memories of Grigori. "He kidnapped my sister's son."

Jace knew she had deliberately avoided answering the question he'd asked, which was to find out what Grigori had done to Abby growing up. Was she hiding from her past, or simply trying to focus attention on the one thing that could still be changed. "Abby—"

She caught his arm, her fingers tight around his wrist. "We have to get him back, Jace."

Jace. The way Abby said his name was like warm rain pouring over him, cleansing the filth from him. She said his name as if he were her salvation, not a monster, not a murderer, not a killer. Something inside him turned over in response to the way she was looking at him, like she saw only the man he'd tried to be, and not the one he'd actually become.

But hell, how could he get involved in this situation? He was a danger to her, and she was a danger to him. He braced his hands on top of his head, watching her, trying to process everything he'd just learned. Her nose was upturned and dainty, but her jaw was jutting out in a determined angle, and her hands were balled into fists by her side.

But this was the daughter of a demon who walked the earth in the form of a man-wolf shifter.

How innocent was she? How innocent could she be? "Do you know the song?" he asked suddenly. He'd been walking down an alley innocently enough when he'd heard that song drifting through an open window. For a split second, he'd been consumed by its beauty, and then it had torn into him, ripping apart his humanity, and igniting a ravenous, killing rage that ripped his wolf from his control, forcing him to shift…and to kill. That same song had turned countless wolves into Grigori's murderous pack. It was the darkest evil, rippling with power. If Abby had grown up in Grigori's pack, she might have access to it. "Do you know the words and the melody?"

Her cheeks turned red. "I do."

He tensed. "So, you could start singing it at any moment and force me to shift?"

Her eyes widened, and her cheeks turned even redder. "I wouldn't do that—"

"But you could." He believed her that she wouldn't do it on purpose. There was a purity to her soul that he felt deep in his bones. He'd never been wrong about a person, and he wasn't worried he was wrong now. But if she had the capacity to turn that song on him…hell. It was a tremendous risk to even be standing near her.

She sighed, but she didn't look away. She met his gaze, and nodded, unwilling to hide the truth from him. "Yes."

"Jesus." He turned away, running his hands through his hair. He'd been living in terror that the song running through his subconscious would force him to shift, and now, here was a woman who could control him with just a whisper. With a few words, she could turn him into a living nightmare over which he had no control.

He realized his hands were shaking, and he shoved them in his pockets to hide his weakness. His index finger hit the silver spheres, and he swore, jerking his hand back when it started to burn.

"Jace!" She grabbed his arm, and he froze, unwilling to turn around to face her. "I'm not like him. My mother died trying to protect us from him. He killed my mother, and he had my sister killed. I despise everything he stands for, including that song. He killed everyone who matters to me." Her voice started to break, and tears swam in her green eyes. "He has my nephew. I have to get him back, Jace. *Please.*"

He steeled himself to her plea, even though her desperation wrenched a part of his soul that he fought so hard to protect. The stakes were too high. He couldn't afford to have emotion interfere. Instead, he replayed that song in his head, the one that had haunted him for weeks, comparing it to her voice. As he did so, a slow burn of dread rose inside him. "Was that *your* voice that I heard singing it? Were *you* the one singing it?"

Stark anguish flashed across her face, giving him his answer.

He stepped back, horrified. "You did that? To your own sister? You had me *kill* her?"

"No!" She reached for him, but he stepped to the right, avoiding her. Instead, she fell to her knees, tears swimming in her eyes. "That was a recording of my voice. I wasn't even there. I just..." She shook her head. "I didn't know my voice could do that, until it was too late. Once Grigori found out, it was too late." She spread her hands, palms up, indicating helplessness. "My own voice killed my sister," she whispered. "It's my fault, Jace. *My fault.*"

Her anguish pierced his shields, and he went down to his knees in front of her. He took her hands, which were ice cold in his. "It's not your fault. He's the murderer, not you." He pressed her hands between his palms, using his shifter heat to warm them. "He wants you, doesn't he?" he asked softly. "You're his weapon. He doesn't want Seth. It's you."

She shook her head. "He doesn't need me anymore. He has my voice recorded. It's Seth, he wants, because Seth is his—" She stopped, cutting herself off.

She didn't need to finish the sentence. He'd already figured it out. "Seth is his grandson."

At her nod, the enormity of the situation pressed down upon him. He was being asked to go rescue Grigori's *grandson*? From Grigori himself? With the woman whose voice could turn him into a murderer? What the fuck?

He wrapped her hands up in his as he fought to process it. He owed Abby and Melissa, but at the same time, the situation was incredibly volatile, fraught with obstacles that risked more innocent deaths. The worst fucking thing he'd done in his life was murder Melissa Stevens, and if he went after Grigori with Abby, he was risking it all again, and so much more.

Abby was with him. She would be his nearest target if he heard the song again, and he had no doubt that Grigori wouldn't hesitate to turn him against Abby, if he decided he didn't need her.

He looked into her desperate green eyes, so full of guilt and self-recrimination, and something inside him roared in response to her vulnerability. He slid his hand along her jaw, tracing the curves of her neck. He needed to help her. He needed to offer her every resource at his disposal...but at the same time, he was bound by what was left of his moral code to protect her from himself.

"Jace?"

He cupped the back of her neck, tangling his fingers in the soft tresses of her hair. "No."

Her face fell, wrenching at his gut. "But—"

"No." He dropped his hand and stood up. "I'm so sorry, Abby. I would do anything for you, except risk your life." Leaving her kneeling in the mud, he forced himself to turn away from her and walked back toward the truck, where Cash and Drake were waiting. "Let's go." He gestured for Cash to move aside so he could open the door, but the shifter didn't move.

"You have to help her," Cash said. "You need to get that kid away from Grigori."

He knew Cash was right, but what the hell? The stakes were too high. "How do I even know what's true and what's not? She could be working for him. I could be walking right into a fucking trap." He didn't want to admit the truth, that he might kill her. He'd led his pack by example, by making them believe that every one of them was stronger than the base instincts of their wolves. It was brutal to have descended into a hell that he'd refused to acknowledge was even real.

"You can scent deceit better than anyone," Cash said. "What did she smell like?"

The faint scent of violet on a summer day brushed

through his mind. "She smelled like warm sunshine and those little purple flowers that come only in the spring," he snapped, blurting it out before he had time to process it. When's Cash's eyes widened in surprise, Jace ground his jaw and glared at him, sort of horrified by what he'd just blurted. Sunshine and flowers? Seriously? She was messing with him, in more ways that he could deal with right now. "Back off, Cash."

"We'll go with you," Cash said. "We'll guard you from her, and we'll protect her from you."

"Yeah, we'll sit between you so there's no hanky-panky," Drake added, grinning. "It'll be like having a chaperone."

"Hanky-panky? What are you, twelve?" The thought of Drake sitting between him and Abby made anger shift inside Jace. He didn't like the idea of the other wolf being next to her. "You can't come," he said, dismissing the idea immediately. "The pack needs you both. We can't leave it unprotected in case Grigori returns."

"Cash can handle the pack. I'll go with you," Drake said. "I won't let you kill her, I swear."

"I can take care of myself," Abby interrupted. There was an audible click, and Jace felt the cold steel of a gun against the back of his neck.

He spun around to find Abby less than a foot away, her gun now pressed to his forehead. "Silver bullets," she said softly. "If you try to kill me, I will take you down." She held up another gun. "This one's for you. If I start to sing, you can kill me."

Cash snorted. "This feels like a safe, supportive partnership with all the makings of a successful pairing."

But Jace didn't laugh. He stared into Abby's unflinching green eyes, and something inside him seemed to settle. She was fully prepared to shoot him, and she was also willing to give him the power to silence her if she started to sing.

"You get it," he said quietly, shocked to realize exactly how deeply entrenched his fear of being forced to shift and kill again was. He could not allow his wolf to kill again. The taste for blood was too intrinsic to the wolf, and the only way to maintain control over it was to never allow it to taste the freedom. His wolf had tasted it once, and now it was ready for more. More death. More slaughter. More merciless killing. If she started to sing, he would have only a split second to react before he would lose control. If he had a gun, that split second would be long enough. But could he shoot her? Was that any better than letting his wolf slaughter someone? Death of an innocent was death, no matter whether it was by a gun or his own slathering jaws.

Pain flashed across her eyes. "I do understand," she said. She held the gun out to him. "Take it. We each get one."

If he took it, he knew he was making a commitment, not just to go after Grigori, but to stop her if she tried to co-opt him. Could he really shoot her? *Really?* He searched her face, and knew the answer was no. His moral code banned using his wolf form to hurt others, but killing a woman in cold blood was different...and equally reprehensible. And specifically, *her.* She called to him in a way no one else had, and he knew he'd give his own life to save hers. Killing her was not an option. "I can't shoot you," he said.

"You can," she said. "I see it in your eyes. You will do whatever it takes to keep yourself from slaughtering anyone else. Your need to keep the world safe is that strong." She leaned forward. "If I were to use my voice to force you to shift and kill, I wouldn't be an innocent worthy of protection, Jace. I would deserve that bullet. I'm not going to sing, but you wouldn't know that yet, so take the gun and keep it, until you know." She held it out again. "Seth's fifth birthday is Saturday."

Shit. The fifth birthday was the first time a wolf could shift. It didn't *have* to shift, but it was capable of it. With the song, Grigori could force a shift that day. He looked at her suddenly. "He'll use your voice to compel him to shift, won't he? He'll play your song for Seth, and then give him prey to slaughter?" If Seth killed the first time he shifted, it would be almost impossible for him to overcome his wolf's taste for blood after that. He'd become a mindless revenant, driven solely by the need to slaughter.

Tears filled her eyes, but she nodded silently, such genuine sadness in her eyes that he knew what he needed to know: he could trust her not to sing to him. He already believed she would shoot him to save herself, which meant that either way, he wasn't at risk of killing her.

Relief flooded him, a relief so deep that his lungs seemed to expand, allowing him to take a deep breath for the first time in what felt like eons. The weight that had been crushing his chest eased, and his shoulders lowered as his tension faded.

It was safe for him to be around her. *Safe.*

"Jace?" She searched his face.

If they didn't act now, that little boy would be facing a lifetime of the hell that Jace had already faced. "I'm in."

She stared at him for a moment, and then a wide smile broke across her face. She threw her arms around his neck and hugged him. For a split second, Jace didn't know what to do. He wasn't used to being hugged, and he felt awkward as hell. She should hate him and fear him on every level.

But when she didn't let go, the heat of her body seemed to soften his resistance. The coldness that had been gripping him so mercilessly since Melissa's death faded, chased away by the warmth she was pouring into him.

Reluctantly, instinctively, his arms folded around her, pulling her against him. She melted into his embrace, pressing her face into the curve of his neck, as if her relief was as great as his. Protectiveness surged through him, and he suddenly understood the burden she carried, of knowing that her voice was being used to murder innocents...including her own sister. That it would be used to turn her own nephew into one of Grigori's blood-crazed disciples.

"No more," he whispered quietly, just to her. "It ends now."

She pulled back, her eyes glistening with tears. "We can't stop Grigori," she said. "He's taken the blood of a vampire, and he's nearly immortal. I just want to get Seth. That's it."

"We'll get him." But as he made the promise, he couldn't help but wonder what happened after that. Grigori had murdered his own daughter to get Seth the first time. What would he do to get him back a second time? Or what would he do to keep him from being taken?

Silently, he wrapped his hands around Abby's, which was still holding her gun. "You have to make me a promise," he said. "If anyone uses that song on me, and I start to shift, you must shoot me." He grasped the gun and pressed the muzzle to his chest, just over his heart. "One shot to end it. You have to swear on your sister's soul that you will not let me be forced to kill again."

Her eyes widened, and she looked down at the gun pressing against his heart.

"I'm an alpha," he said. "No wolf can stop me if I get in a killing frenzy. *No one.* I'm that fucking good. So, you have to promise. A silver bullet to the heart would stop me, but it has to be in the heart." He paused. "How well can you shoot?"

"I've trained for hundreds of hours. I never miss." She searched his face, and he allowed her to see into his soul, into the blackened, shriveled remains of his soul. He wanted her to argue with him, to say that she could tell he was a good man, one who would never fall down that fucking rabbit hole again. He wanted her to believe in him when he'd already proven that he wasn't worth believing in.

He wanted her to protest, to say that she could see it in his soul that he would be strong enough to resist the song that she knew so well.

But she didn't. Her eyes glistened with new tears, but she nodded. "Okay. I promise to shoot you. Let's go."

Chapter Four

THREE HOURS LATER, Abby was no longer sure she'd made the right choice. Jace had felt the place to start their search was the last place Seth had been, which was her sister's apartment. It had seemed like a good idea at the time, but as they rounded the corner of the hallway that led to the abandoned apartment, Abby's hands began to shake, and she paused. Sweat trickled down her spine, and fear knotted her belly.

Jace, who was already at the door of the apartment, glanced back at her. He frowned, then walked back over to her, even his innate grace unable to hide the pain that shocked his system each time he put weight on his broken ankle. "What's wrong?" he asked softly, his voice so quiet that no one else would hear it, no matter who might be around.

"Nothing." She wiped her hands on her jeans, trying not to notice how much they were trembling. "I'm fine."

He raised his eyebrows. "You're afraid of Grigori."

"He was here," she blurted out. "He was in this hallway, maybe right in this very spot, waiting for you to attack my sister so he could grab Seth. I just—I just feel like he's here now, waiting, just like before."

"Hey." Jace took her hand, pressing her palm between his, a gesture she was already beginning to recognize as his way of connecting with her and letting her know that he was on her side. She took a deep breath, focusing on the strength and warmth of his hands as they dwarfed hers. "I know his scent. He's not here." He smiled. "Plus, he'd never make it that easy, right?"

She swallowed, gripping his hands. "I know, but it just...it freaks me out that he was here, right where I'm standing."

"I know." He pushed a strand of hair back from her face, his touch gentle, so much softer than she would ever have expected from him. "You need to understand something about me," he said softly. "I don't believe in killing. I work hard to teach my pack how to control their wolves. I believe compassion brings out the best in people, not force."

She nodded. "I can tell." She'd felt his kindness the first moment she'd heard his voice when he'd been talking to her grandmother. She knew he was different from Grigori, and from all the others. That was why she'd asked him for help. Never would she have gone near him if she'd sensed any of the depravity or violence she'd grown up around. "But—"

"No." He touched his index finger to her lips, silencing her. "I'm not finished. What you need to understand is that I *never* confuse compassion with weakness. As an alpha, I've done whatever it takes to keep my wolves safe, including kill those who needed to be killed. I don't do it for pleasure. I do it as a protector, and my wolf knows the difference. I'm stronger, faster, and more ruthless than anyone." His eyes darkened. "You're under my protection, Abby. I will do whatever it takes to protect you from him, and I can do a great deal."

A wave of heat rushed over her, the powerful surge of his energy as his wolf paced beneath the surface. Her heart stuttered in response to the sheer dominance he gave off. This wasn't the shifter who'd gone down on his knees in submission to her grandmother. This was the alpha who had strung together a pack of misfits and made them honorable, admirable, and so strong that no one had dared try to take them over...no one except Grigori. He was pure power, and he was offering it to her. "That's why Grigori chose you, isn't it?" she asked. "Because you're so powerful, right? He wants to dominate you, because you're the only one strong enough to stop him."

He pressed his lips together, and something passed across his face, an evasiveness that told her that she was wrong. "Partially."

She stiffened. He'd been selected for another reason, a reason he wasn't planning to share. "What haven't you told me, Jace?"

He grimaced. "I was orphaned as a young boy when my parents were killed in a car crash. I was thrown from the car and left to die, but Grigori's father found me and brought me into the pack."

Abby stared at him, shocked by his revelation. "You were in their pack?"

"For six months. The first day I was recovered enough to leave my bed, I was in the woods, testing my leg, when I came across his father training some of the wolves in his pack."

Abby's stomach turned. She'd seen that training. Most wolves didn't survive it. "What happened?"

"I tried to stop him." Jace shrugged. "Grigori's dad kicked my ass, and turned me over to Grigori to kill."

It didn't surprise her at all that Jace had tried to interfere, even when he was a young boy and hopelessly outmatched. "But you're alive." Understanding dawned. "You defeated him, didn't you? And he hates you for it?"

He nodded. "I'd heard the pack had been exterminated, but apparently, I was wrong."

"So, isn't he hunting you, now? You got out of jail. He didn't win." She knew how Grigori worked. The fact that Jace was suffering inside would be worthless to him. He wouldn't stop until Jace was destroyed.

"I've tried to find him, but I can't. I think he's gone underground to develop a new plan." Jace narrowed his eyes. "I'll be ready this time. So will my pack." His eyes darkened. "That day defined who I was. I made it my mission to protect wolves from bastards like Grigori's father. I resolved never to allow my wolf to be like them, and I never have. Until your sister."

She understood now. "That's why he used the song on you, isn't it? He wanted you to become that which you've crusaded against."

"He wanted me to become him." Jace narrowed his eyes. "I won't let him win. No matter what, I will *never* become like the monster I saw that day."

She knew he spoke the truth. His honor was stamped in every line of his body, in every word he spoke, in the way his fingers curved protectively around hers, offering her all he was to keep her safe. The fear that had been suffocating her dissolved, replaced by a feeling of security. Jace was unlike any other male she'd ever known, and she was safe as long as she was with him. "You're incredible," she said softly.

He grinned. "I used to think so, but I'm a little more realistic now." His smile faded and he brushed his knuckles across her jaw. "It gives me hope that you see me that way. I need that."

She tilted her head into his touch. "Me, too."

For a moment, neither of them said anything. It was just a silent, powerful connection between two people who had seen hell and found their way out, half-broken, but somehow still breathing. In his presence, her fear of Grigori faded, replaced by something new and stronger. They'd both survived so much of Grigori's hell. Why couldn't they win one more time?

Something flashed in Jace's eyes. Pain? Guilt? Empathy? "Did you ever live with him?" he asked quietly, his gaze searching hers. "With Grigori?"

She shrugged with the nonchalance that had become her escape from the bitterness of her past. "Until I was seventeen."

"Seventeen." Jace repeated her answer, his eyes glittering. Anger surged in his face, and for a split second, his eyes shifted to the gray-green of his wolf. She sucked in her breath, but he'd regained control before she could even be sure she'd seen it.

He took her hands, his fingers closing on hers. "I won't let him take you again," he said, his voice like steel. "I swear it."

Tears filled her eyes at his fierce words. She wasn't used to someone standing by her side, offering his protection to her. She was so used to being on her own, learning how to fight, to protect herself for the day when Grigori decided to turn his depravity onto her. "It's not about me," she said. "It's about Seth. If you have to choose between us, get him free, not me. I promised my sister."

Jace slipped his hand through her hair, tangling his fingers in the locks that hung over her shoulder, his gaze searching hers. "So brave. Willing to sacrifice yourself to protect another," he whispered, his voice almost reverent. "Such honor in you."

She shook her head. "No, I'm just doing what's right. Seth is still innocent. He deserves a chance to live."

"You're not *just* anything," he interrupted, his voice steely with anger. "Don't let anyone tell you that you are. You're selfless, honorable, and brave, even when you're terrified." His fingers tightened in her hair, and suddenly her breath caught, and she froze. "You're a hell of a woman, Abby."

His gaze went to her mouth, and anticipation raced through her. Was he going to *kiss* her?

"Jace?" she whispered, swallowing as his gaze darkened. Her heart started to hammer. Why was he looking at her like that?

He lifted his gaze to hers, his eyes stark with desperate longing. She saw in them the depth of suffering in his soul, the gaping chasm that was sucking him down, the absolute self-hate for what he'd done to her sister. He was a drowning man, sucked into a miasma of hell and damnation that Grigori had plunged him into. She'd seen suffering in her life, plenty of it, but never had she felt the depths of pain that was tormenting him.

"Jace." She grasped the front of his jacket, as if she could hold his head above water and keep him from sinking into the quagmire forever. She wanted to hold him, to kiss him, to do whatever it took to save him from his own hell, one that he'd been plunged into because of her song, and her voice.

His fingers tightened in her hair, a grasp that was almost desperate. "There's so little honor left in this world," he whispered, his voice raw and hoarse. "So little beauty. So little to believe in. Until you."

Her heart seemed to stutter in her chest. No one had ever looked at her with such intensity. No one had ever spoken words like that, words so rich with emotion that they seemed to fill the air between them. "Jace—"

A thump from the apartment made them both jump, breaking the moment. Jace spun away from her, shoving her behind him as he faced the door.

There was another thud, and he leapt toward the door, moving with such speed and agility that she thought he'd actually partially shifted as he moved. He reached the door, kicked it open and charged inside, not even hesitating for a split second.

There was a loud crash, a violent snarl, and then silence.

Abby pulled her gun free and pointed it at the door, her heart thundering. She'd lied to Jace when she'd bragged about her gun skills. She was a sharpshooter when it came to inanimate targets, but never once had she managed to put a bullet into a living creature, not even to save her own mother's life. The gun was for show, a facade that would be exposed the moment someone called her on it. "Jace?" she whispered, her voice quivery.

There were no sounds from the room.

Should she call the police? Go into the room?

Damn it.

She couldn't risk calling the police. What if something had happened? Neither of them could afford to be tied down by police bureaucracy, especially Jace, who'd just gotten exonerated from murder charges, a result that most of the people in the city didn't agree with.

Slowly, her heart thundering so loudly she could barely hear above the pounding, she edged down the hallway, her shoulder pressed against the wall. "Jace?" she whispered again, knowing that the shifter could hear her easily.

No response.

Crud. What had happened in there?

She reached the doorway, but just pressed herself against the wall, unable to make herself leap into the doorway as Jace had done. She took a deep breath, then peeked around the doorframe into the apartment.

China fragments were shattered on the floor, tinged with blood, but there was no sign of Jace. She gripped the gun more tightly, scanning the one-room apartment. The window above the fire escape was open, just like it had been the day her sister had died, and suddenly her heart seemed to congeal. What had happened to Jace? How could he just disappear like that?

Was this a set up? Had Grigori been waiting for her to come back? Had it all been—

The skin on the back of her neck prickled suddenly, but before she could turn, a hand clamped over her mouth, and she was pulled up against a hard body. "Welcome back, Abigail."

Oh, God. *Lucius Stevens.* Her sister's husband. She went cold with terror, and for a split second, she forgot how to breathe, as the familiar voice of Grigori's beta slithered over her like a knife blade. The scars on her stomach from his teeth burned with the reminder of the night he'd attacked her as punishment for standing in the way of what he'd wanted. *He* was involved? She'd thought he was dead. She'd thought this was about Grigori. Dear God, not *Lucius.*

"Get inside the apartment," he said, his finger sliding down her wrist and around her gun, prying it from her stiff fingers.

God, no. She could never go anywhere with him. Death was better than being in his hands. As terrified as she was of Grigori, it was Lucius who haunted her nightmares.

His fingers tightened around her neck, and he pressed his body into her, forcing her forward. She knew she couldn't go into the apartment with him. She couldn't be alone with him. Never again. "No!" She flung herself backwards, slamming the back of her head into his throat. He gagged and stumbled back, releasing her.

"Jace! Help!" She spun around and raced past Lucius, her feet flying as she tore down the hall and hurtled down the steps toward the street. She had to get outside. She had to get to the car. She had to get where there were witnesses. She had to find Jace—

Lucius tackled her, his lithe body shoving her down the stairs. She screamed, grabbing for the railing as she catapulted forward. Her fingers slipped off the slick wood, flailing through empty air as she lunged for it again, the scream lodged in her throat—

Lucius leapt past her and reached the landing below a split second before she did. He caught her just before she hit, and hauled her against him. His ruthless eyes bore down at her, as he fisted her hair and yanked her head back. "Did you really think I'd let you die?" he snapped. "There's so much to do before you get that reprieve, Abigail."

He raised his lips in a snarl, and she saw his face and incisors start to lengthen. She screamed and tried to slam her knee into his groin, but he was ready this time. His arms were like steel bands as he locked her against his body. He shifted partially, with the head of a wolf and the body of a man, a feat that should have been impossible. For a split second, she was too horrified to struggle, and then, too late, she saw his teeth coming for her throat.

She had no time to react before his teeth sank into her neck.

Chapter Five

ABBY'S SCREAM KNIFED through Jace's subconscious, jerking him awake. He lunged to his feet, then swore as he went down, his head spinning with dizziness. Swearing, he touched his head, gritting his jaw when he felt the open wound from the hit he'd taken. Someone had knocked him out with a single blow when he'd burst into the apartment. What the hell was going on? He hadn't seen or heard anyone before being struck. He'd just come through the door and been hit from behind. How had his assailant evaded detection?

Abby screamed again, jerking his focus off his injuries. Jace spun around, swiftly assessing the situation. He was in an alley, the same alley where he'd attacked Melissa, just outside her apartment. The air was filled with the scent of wolf, a scent he didn't recognize, a wolf that had apparently attacked him and then dumped him. It was mingled with Abby's scent, and it was coming from the apartment. "Abby!" He tried to take a step, but pain exploded through him, dragging him down to his knees.

He twisted around and saw his ankle was locked in a bear trap, the rusted teeth deep in his already injured ankle, blood oozing from his boot. The moment he saw it, pain ratcheted through his whole body, a searing, burning pain that made every muscle tremble with weakness. Who the fuck had he run into in that apartment?

Swearing, he grabbed the jaws of the trap and tried to pry them apart, but it was impossible. The sheer force of them was too great, crushing the bones in his ankle. He closed his eyes and summoned the wolf he'd fought so hard to suppress ever since he'd killed Melissa. Greedy for power, his wolf surged, ripping him from his human form with breathless ferocity. The split second his leg shifted, Jace jerked it free of the trap in the millisecond before the jaws closed on his smaller, wolf leg.

Shedding his clothes, he lurched to his feet and broke into a three-legged sprint, hurtling down the alley he'd had so many nightmares about. He shoved aside the guilt, focusing on Abby. He raced up the fire escape and leapt through the open window of the apartment. He paused long enough to scent Abby, and then followed it out the door. He tore through the open doorway and down the hall to the exit.

He slammed his shoulder into the stairwell door, and it flew open. The moment he entered the stairwell, the scent of fresh blood assaulted him. *Abby's blood.* His wolf roared with fury, and he sprinted down the stairs, every muscle tensed as he rounded the corner of the landing. At the bottom of the stairs, a man with a wolf head was bent over Abby, his jaws wrapped around her throat.

Jace vaulted off the top step, howling his challenge

as he leapt. The wolf raised his head, his white teeth pink with her blood. The moment he saw Jace, he shoved Abby aside and whirled toward Jace, his lips curled in a menacing snarl.

Jace twisted in midair, evading the wolf's bite, and then sank his teeth into the soft flesh of his arm, which was still in its vulnerable human form. The wolf snarled and shifted, but it was too late. Jace's grip was too tight, too secure, his teeth buried deep. Blood poured from the wound into Jace's mouth, igniting a raw, primal hunger, feeding the wolf he'd contained for so long.

Bloodlust poured through him, and his gaze shifted to a scarlet-haze. The need to kill raged through him, and he bit deeper, searching for the artery that would bleed his victim out in minutes.

"Jace," Abby's desperate whisper broke through the frenzied hunger in his mind. Protectiveness surged through him, tearing his wolf's focus from destruction to preservation. He had to break away. He had to help her. But his wolf was too focused on the kill. He wouldn't be diverted—

The half-man kicked Jace's injured leg.

Pain screamed through him, shocking his body into agonizing pain. Jace lost his grip on his victim, falling to the ground as his muscles convulsed in agony.

"Jace!"

Abby! He lurched to his feet and spun around. She was curled on her side, gripping the front of her neck. Her face was ashen, but her eyes were bright and alive. "Your leg," she whispered.

He knew about his leg. Yeah, he fucking *knew* about it.

The half-wolf lunged to his feet and Jace whipped

around to face him as he finished shifting into full wolf form...a massive black wolf that outweighed Jace by at least twenty pounds. Jace positioned himself in front of Abby as he raised his lips in a snarl.

The black wolf went into the same position, its silver eyes gleaming with the thrill of the fight. His weight was evenly spread on all four legs, and the wound Jace had inflicted upon him appeared to be healing already. He was pure muscle and menace, eager to kill, ready to fight to the end.

Jace knew he had to hide his injury, but his leg was dangling uselessly. There was literally no way he could put his foot down, and the other wolf knew it. Jace's entire body was shaking with the effort of holding himself upright. He was losing blood fast, and the sheer magnitude of the injury was so extreme he couldn't block the pain as well as he needed to. His body was starting to go into shock, and he knew he had to fight to stay in control.

Ruthlessly, Jace shoved the injury aside, summoning every last shred of discipline he possessed to keep his body functioning. The other wolf began to circle around him. Jace turned with it, keeping himself between the wolf and Abby. *Get to the car,* he ordered her, unsure whether she would be able to hear him. He communicated with his pack telepathically when he was in wolf form, but Abby was completely human.

But she rolled to her side, and started to crawl toward the door, as if she'd heard him.

The wolf's silver eyes flicked toward Abby, and Jace saw the glint of possessiveness in the animal. He knew then, without a doubt, that the wolf would not let her go. Abby was personal to him. What the hell was going on?

Jace growled to get his attention off Abby, and the wolf looked back at him, his gaze going to Jace's dangling leg. He turned toward Jace again and raised his lips in a silent snarl. He was going in for the kill, and they both knew that Jace, with his injured leg, had no chance against him.

Fuck. This wasn't how it was supposed to go down. He didn't give a shit if he died, but if he died, it meant Abby had no protection against this bastard. He crouched low, protecting his belly, teeth bared as he prepared for the attack. His only chance would be to come from underneath and latch onto a soft, unprotected part. It was risky, but he had no choice. One more hit to his leg, and he'd be unable to continue. As it was, his muscles were shaking violently, barely able to contain the pain.

The black wolf tensed to spring and—

*S*irens suddenly screamed in the distance. Both wolves froze, listening. The black wolf snarled, then spun away. He scooped up his clothes in his teeth, then bolted out the door, disappearing from sight as his toenails clicked on the asphalt as he deserted the scene.

Jace immediately collapsed on the hard floor, unable to hold himself up for a moment longer.

"Jace!" Abby leapt to her feet. "We need to get out of here."

Her urgency pierced his veil of pain. She was right. They had to leave. Now. Swearing, he tried to stand, but his body gave out on him. Desperation raged through him as Abby hurried over, blood oozed from the bite marks in her neck. Son of a bitch. He had to get her out of there. With his history, the cops would lock him up, and there was no way he was going to leave her unprotected while he rotted behind bars.

With a surge of energy, he forced himself to shift back to his human form. He bellowed with agony as the bones, muscles, and tendons in his crushed leg shifted, collapsing again as his body fought to hold itself together. *Holy fuck.*

Abby crouched beside him, her face stark with pain and fear. "Are you okay?"

The sirens were getting louder. "Fantastic." His voice raw, he grabbed the railing and hauled himself to his feet. He was naked, covered in blood, with a woman who had wolf bites on her neck...and the police were coming. They had to bail, but if she was in danger of dying, he was going to make her stay so the paramedics could save her. "Let me see."

She didn't hesitate. She just pulled her hand from her neck. "I'm okay."

His gut went cold when he saw the wounds. They were deep and raw, the marks of a dominant wolf trying to punish. Her fragile skin had been marked and torn...but it hadn't been a killing bite. She was marked, but barely bleeding. Satisfied she wasn't in danger at the moment, he nodded. "Okay, let's go."

She slung his arm over her shoulder, supporting his injured side. "Hurry."

He used her only for balance, refusing to burden her with his weight as he hopped across the floor, every movement sending shards of pain through him. Sweat trickled down his back in rivulets, the pain so great he could barely stay conscious. He knew it shouldn't hurt that badly, but he didn't have time to assess it. They had to get away first.

"Lean on me, Jace." She ordered as they slipped outside to the alley where he'd left his SUV.

"No." If he leaned on her, he'd impede both of their

movements. She needed to be able to run, and he need-ed to be able to fight. But son of a bitch, he'd never felt pain like this before. It wasn't only in his ankle. It was everywhere in his body, as if his blood was literally burning him up from the inside.

He stumbled and she caught him. He fought for balance, but soon she was half-dragging him across the alley toward his truck. The sirens were screaming now, almost upon them.

"Get in!" She pulled open the passenger door, and he fell onto the seat, barely able to drag his injured leg into the car.

"My keys," he gasped. "They're in my pants. In the alley. Near the fire escape."

"Got it!" She flung the door shut and raced away.

Jace leaned back against the seat, fighting for breath, focusing on the pain and willing it out of his body. It wasn't only about the pain, however. He could tell that his ankle was absolutely pulverized. The bones had turned to dust, the tendons and muscles shredded. It was so far beyond what he could heal, even as a shifter. He knew it would never heal. There was no way he could be an alpha, or survive in his world on three legs. Weakness would be exploited, and he would be targeted. "Fuck!"

Abby opened the driver's door, and flung his clothes at him. She jammed the keys into the ignition and the engine roared to life. She hit the gas and the SUV leapt forward, the tires spinning on the dirty alley floor. Jace gritted his teeth as he slid across the seat, his ankle bumping against the side of the car.

The car flew out of the alley, skidding as she turned right on the main road. Jace twisted around in his seat, watching the street behind them. Just as she turned the car around the next corner, the police cars came into view, screaming to a stop in front of the apartment building.

As Abby drove, he kept watching behind them, waiting for the cops to come after them...but they didn't. After five minutes, he realized they were safe.

With a low groan, he finally turned around and sank into the seat. He was still naked, bloody, and broken, but he didn't give a shit. His clothes were in a pile on his lap, and that was all the modesty she was going to get. "We're good." His adrenaline began to fade, leaving him with no protection against the pain. He closed his eyes, gritting his teeth. His mind was spinning now, fragmenting as it tried to defend against the utter destruction of his leg.

"You need a hospital," she said. "They'll have to operate."

"No. They'll put in steel plates and pins. I'll never be able to shift again."

"But—"

He opened his eyes to look at her. "No."

She pressed her lips together. "You think being a crippled shifter is better than being a healed man?"

"Yeah, I do." He watched her drive through half-lidded eyes. "If I hadn't been able to shift today, that black wolf would have you right now. So, yeah, it's better. My world is the shifter world, not the human one." He closed his eyes again, needing to focus all his energy on his leg. "I need time to try to heal it as best I can. We'll go to my place. It's safe." He gave her his address, gritting his teeth when the car hit a bump. "Can you get us there?"

"Of course." She looked over at him. "You should wrap your ankle. It's..." She grimaced. "God, Jace, it looks horrible."

"It's fine." She was right, though. He needed to stabilize it. With a groan he couldn't suppress, he grabbed his tee shirt and tore it into strips. He leaned over to wrap his ankle, but the moment his fingers touched it, he almost doubled over from the pain. "Son of a bitch." He'd been bitten dozens of times in his life. He'd had wounds that should have killed him, but nothing had hurt like his leg. It was as if all the broken fragments kept shifting position, igniting new shards of pain.

Or maybe it hurt so much because he knew he wasn't going to be able to heal it properly. The loss of his leg was as agonizing as the pain itself. It wasn't like getting his gut ripped open. He could heal that. But his ankle? He'd seen shifters with injuries like his, and they never healed sufficiently. He'd never be able to do what he needed to do again. But he was going to try. He was damned good at healing, and he wasn't going to give up easily. If he could regain even partial use of it, that would help. But he knew he'd never have the agility he once had. It was over, forever.

"Do you want me to splint it?" she asked.

"No." Shit, no. He wasn't that weak. With a growl of determination, he jerked the strip of his tee shirt around his ankle, wrapping it tightly. White spots swam before his eyes, but he didn't stop. He just wrapped the fucking thing like a mummy, until his ankle was swathed in a bloodstained tourniquet that would do nothing to actually heal it, but might support it enough for him to walk if he needed to.

He leaned back against the seat, sweat beading from every pore in his body. He closed his eyes, knowing he needed to sleep, but unwilling to leave Abby unprotected. "Who was he?" he asked. "The black wolf. He knew you. It was personal." When she didn't answer, he looked over at her. Her face was pale, and there were dark circles under her eyes.

Protectiveness surged through him, propelled by a dark sense of foreboding. Instinctively, he scanned their surroundings, making sure no one was following him...but he'd done that at the apartment, and he hadn't sensed the black wolf. "Talk to me, Abby. What don't I know?"

"I thought he was dead," she whispered. She glanced over at him, her eyes wide with the kind of fear that made outrage pour through him. "He was supposed to be dead."

"Who?"

"He...." She swallowed. "He's my sister's husband. Seth's father."

Son of a bitch. His *father*?

Taking on Grigori, who'd claimed the boy as his own kin was bad enough. But to add on a wolf protecting his own *son*? Jesus.

They were fucked.

* * *

Abby looked over at Jace, who had fallen into a fitful, painful sleep while she drove. He'd put on his leather jacket, but his skin was cold and ashen, and his energy was low. His ankle looked like it was destroyed. When he'd wrapped it, it had virtually crumbled beneath the bandages. Had his bones basically turned to dust from the two injuries? How could an alpha wolf survive on three legs? How would he defeat Grigori? After Lucius's trap and Jace's story about his past with Grigori, she knew they were both being hunted. It was simply a matter of whether she and Jace were caught before they found Seth. Either way, they were going to meet. When they did, someone would win, and someone would die.

She gripped the steering wheel, desperately trying to decide what to do about Jace. If she did nothing, he would be on three legs his whole life, a weakened state that would turn him into the hunted by other wolves. There was one person who might be able to help him, but he was from her past, the time when Grigori knew her.

Would Grigori guess she would go there?

He might.

But if she didn't... She touched her neck, grimacing at the torn skin. It wasn't a deadly bite, but it was significant. She was afraid of what Lucius had done to her. So deeply afraid.

How big was the risk if she asked for help? How significant was the impact if she didn't?

If she asked for help, they had a chance to survive. It was possible it would pay off.

If she didn't ask for help, it was guaranteed they would have no chance when Grigori or Lucius found them. What choice did she have?

None. Because hiding wasn't an option. Somewhere out there was Seth, four years old, in the hands of a madman that would strip him of his humanity within days. She had to seek out help, and just be very, very careful while she was there.

She looked over at Jace, then put on her blinker to turn off the main road, away from his house, away from the place he'd told her to go, and to the one destination he'd probably never agree to go.

As the truck bumped over the dirt road, she prayed she'd made the right choice.

If Lucius and Grigori were waiting for her when they arrived, the ending would come too fast, and they would lose.

Chapter Six

THREE HOURS LATER, Abby emerged from the winding dirt road, slowing the SUV when she saw the familiar cabin hidden in the shadows of the tall pine trees. The shutters were askew. Vines had grown over the windows. Weeds owned the walkway. The windows were cracked, and no light shined from within. It looked like no one had set foot in there for decades.

Relief rushed through her. *Kiernan still lived there.*

Warily, she pulled up in front of the cabin and turned the engine off. She scanned the woods around them, searching the shadows for any indications that Grigori or Lucius was waiting for her, but she didn't see any sign of them. The birds were chirping, the squirrels were bustling about, and all the forest creatures were acting normally, which they wouldn't if there was a wolf shifter in their midst.

She let out a deep sigh of relief, realizing that the first hurdle had been passed, for now.

"We're here?" Jace opened his eyes, and looked sleepily around. His entire body tensed, and he sat up quickly, sucking in his breath when he accidentally moved his leg. "Where are we?"

"A friend's place." Maybe a friend. Maybe an enemy. "He might be able to help. He's a gifted healer." Abby started to open her door, but Jace lunged across her, his hand clamping down on hers.

His grip was like steel, his silver eyes glittering with fury. "Don't open the door," he snapped. "We're leaving."

Despite his injury, power thrummed through him. His muscles were taut, his body a deadly machine. Awareness rippled through her, a deep awareness of exactly what kind of man he was. Despite his warning, she had mistaken his guilt and his injury for weakness. She'd seen him as a victim who needed help.

He wasn't.

He was pure alpha, and he was pissed. Heat rose from his body where he was leaning across her, his abdominal muscles hard and unyielding where he was pressed against her belly, pinning her to the seat.

She swallowed, her heart starting to pound at the intimacy of their position. It had been so long since she'd noticed a man, so long since she'd responded to one. Now was not the time, but there was something about Jace that shattered her shields and dragged her mercilessly under his spell. "Jace—"

His gaze went to hers, and something shifted in the air, something that turned intensely sexual, making heat lick through her body. She caught her breath, aware that his upper arm was against her breast, and he hadn't moved it away.

For a long moment, he didn't move, and neither did she. Tension hovered between them, heated, dangerous, and loaded. There was so much at stake, and yet she couldn't tear her gaze off his. Her entire body seemed to be wound into a tight knot of fire and heat, held in abeyance by the barest thread of self-control.

His gaze went to her mouth, then snapped back up to her face almost instantly, but the heat continued to rise from his body. "We're not safe here," he said, his low voice wrapping around her like an invisible caress. "Drive us out of here."

She swallowed, knowing it must be making him crazy that his injured ankle kept him from driving. "You can't heal your ankle on your own."

"I'm fine—"

"And I'm worried about my bite," she blurted out.

His gaze went to her throat, his brow furrowing as he inspected it. He still hadn't retreated, his body pressing her into the seat. "It's not deep—"

"It's not my first one from him." It was almost impossible for someone to become a shifter just from being bitten by one. But repeated, grievous injury from the same wolf was a different story, with the potential to turn the human into a shifter. Not all females with one shifter parent inherited the ability to shift. When it became apparent that she was one of those failures, Grigori had ordered Lucius to turn her into one by biting her repeatedly until the wolf proteins built up in her blood. She'd fought it desperately, because a bitten shifter always became a half-crazed werewolf, unable to contain their bloodlust. Those shifters were the ones that horrors of werewolf lore were founded upon.

His face darkened. "*What*?" His voice was clipped, taut with fury.

Crud. She hadn't meant to tell him. She didn't need his sympathy. All she wanted was to get out of the SUV and find Kiernan, praying that he would help.

"Nothing. I just—"

His gaze went to her stomach, and she realized she'd pressed her hand over her old wounds. She winced as understanding flashed across his face. Damn him for being perceptive.

Scowling, he grasped the waistband of her shirt and started to pull it up.

She grabbed his wrist, holding his hand down, panic rippling through her. "No, don't."

No one ever got to see her stomach, and the last thing she could endure was Jace being the first one to see her truth.

* * *

Jace froze at the sudden fear in Abby's eyes when he grasped the hem of her shirt.

Her face had paled, and her grip on his wrist was desperate. Her fingernails were digging into his skin. Swearing under his breath, he went still, trying not to threaten her. She looked so vulnerable that his alpha protective instincts surged to the surface. He would not hurt her. He had to keep her safe. "Let me see," he said, keeping his voice gentle, letting her hear the strength he was offering her.

She shook her head. "No." She dismissed him quickly. "It's fine—"

"Abby. This is my world. I need to know." Foreboding was pressing heavily at him, the certainty that something was very wrong, that she'd been hiding so much from him. "Let me see," he said again.

Her eyes narrowed. "You're a persistent pain in the ass."

He grinned. "Yeah, I am."

"Fine, but only because I don't want to listen to

your harassment for the next hour." She glared at him one more time, then she bit her lower lip and let her fingers slide off his wrist. Her bravado faded into vulnerability as she clasped her hands on top of her head and stared out the windshield, avoiding eye contact with him.

His heart softened at her stoic resignation, and he touched her jaw lightly to reassure her and connect them. The moment his fingers brushed over her skin, he went still, shocked by how soft her skin was. So fragile, so smooth, so delicate. Fierce protectiveness roared through him, a need to draw her into his inner circle and offer her the protection he was born to give.

Her gaze flicked toward him, and for a moment, time was suspended again. Every time he got close to her, he was trapped by the sheer intensity of his response to her. He was aware of her on every level as a woman. Every part of who he was responded to her. He needed to touch her, be with her, help her, and even claim her... except he had no right. He'd brought only hell and damnation upon her and her family. There was no way he was ever going to consider himself worthy of touching her the way he burned to.

But protecting her was different. That was what defined him: guardianship and preservation of those who had no other defenses, even if their most savage enemy was themselves. He'd fallen into the role of an alpha after rescuing assorted wayward shifters who were headed in bad directions. Killing Melissa had violated everything that mattered to him, and he owed everything to the woman in his arms.

Keeping his gaze on Abby's face, he gently clasped the hem of her shirt and tugged it upward. Her lips pressed together, but she didn't look away from his face, making his heart twist. She was looking at him like a cornered wolf pup, willing to trust him, but ready to fight back if she was proven wrong to put her faith in him.

"I'm not going to hurt you," he repeated as he pulled her shirt up to her breasts.

Her lips tightened, and she shrugged. "Whatever." Her nonchalance was superficial, hiding emotion she was determined not to share with him.

Damn. The damage ran deep in her, and it pissed him off. Gritting his jaw, he tore his gaze off hers and looked down at her stomach.

What he saw made fury thunder through him. Her skin was a mass of brutal, devastating scars that went from her breasts to below the waistband of her jeans. How was she still alive? "Son of a bitch, Abby. What happened to you?" But she didn't need to answer him. He knew. The crisscross of old scars were made by teeth, the deep, grievous injury of a wolf shifter trying to disembowel its prey. A fierce, white-hot rage burned through him, fury at what she'd suffered. His need to protect her deepened to a pulsating, powerful compulsion that radiated all the way from the depths of his soul.

He flattened his hand across the scars, as if he could shield her body from the attack that had happened so long ago. The skin was hard and ridged beneath his palms, stretched taut over the injuries. "Jesus, Abby," he said softly. "I'm so sorry."

She slipped her fingers through his hair, and he looked up. Tears were glistening in her eyes, tears that tore past his shields and plunged deep inside him. Swearing, he pressed his hand to her cheeks and brushed his thumb over a tear that trickled free. "I'm sorry," he said again.

A small smile flickered across her face, and she tightened her fingers in his hair. "The few times someone has seen my stomach, they've been repulsed by the ugliness of the scars, and by the horror of the incident that caused them. Everyone retreats, both physically and emotionally...but you didn't." She put her hand on his, which was still spread across her belly. "You touched me like you were trying to heal them and protect me. You poured warmth into me. You looked at me like...you still saw *me*."

He frowned. "Of course I see you. I already know you're courageous and loyal. Your ability to forgive is unheralded. Those scars were someone's attempt to destroy you, and you didn't let them. You're tough as hell, Abby, but at the same time, there's a kindness to you that still burns brightly despite everything." A wave of regret washed over him. "You deserve so much more than what I did to your family," he said quietly. "I know I can't make it right, but you have my oath that I will stand beside you and fight until you don't need me anymore."

She searched his face. "And then you'll kill yourself, won't you?"

He shrugged, not even caring about his future. Right now, all that mattered was Abby. "My duty is to others. If I'm not safe to be around, then it's my job to address that fact."

She sighed, tracing her finger along his jaw. He closed his eyes, focusing on the sensation of her touch. As the pack alpha, he never showed weakness or softness, and no one ever offered it to him...until this moment. Until Abby touched his face so gently that he felt himself falling into the magic she wove around him.

For a brief, fierce moment, he wished he'd never become an alpha. He wished he'd somehow found a life where a moment like this one was his reality, something he deserved, something he could have for more than a millisecond in his life.

"What if I could help you with that?" she asked.

"With what? Making this moment last forever?" Shit. Had he really just said that? He snapped his eyes open, and she was staring at him with a shocked look on her face.

Yeah, so apparently, he had just said that. Damn. He had no place fantasizing about that kind of shit. Swearing, he pulled back, reclaiming his side of the SUV. "Let's get going," he said, his voice rougher than he'd intended. "Back to my place. I don't like being out here."

She didn't move. "What if I could teach you to be stronger than the song? That's what I meant."

He went still, his entire body snapping into hypervigilance at the mention of the song that controlled him. "What do you mean?" he asked cautiously.

"Desensitization. I can sing it and you can practice resisting—"

"No!" He lunged across the seat and pressed his hand to her belly, pinning her to the seat. "Do you feel those scars?" he asked. "Do you? Because I can do so much worse than that. That song unleashed a monster inside me, and if you are *anywhere* near me when it happens, you're dead. Do you get it? *Dead.*"

"You're not like him," she said, her voice steady, not pulling away from his touch. "You're different."

"So different that I killed your sister? Your fucking *sister*, Abby. How can you forget that? I'm the monster. *I am the monster.*"

She didn't pull away. No look of horror crossed her face. In fact...she almost looked empathetic. "Jace—"

"Fuck this. Just fuck this." Why couldn't she understand how dangerous he was? Jace shoved open his car door and stepped out, keeping all his weight on his uninjured foot. He slammed the door behind him and leaned against the SUV. He clasped his hands on top of his head and took a deep breath, trying to calm down.

Didn't she see him for what he was? How on earth could she possibly suggest she sing that cursed song to him? She might believe that he could build an immunity to the song, but he knew better. He'd been inside his body when his wolf had taken over. He'd tasted the blood and wanted more. He'd stared into the eyes of her sister while he'd stolen her life, and he'd felt the primal roar of pleasure from his wolf. He'd heard the distant screams of horror from his soul, trying to stop the carnage, and he'd felt the deep satisfaction of his wolf when he'd crushed that pathetic spark of rebellion.

He was the one who'd lived through the moment when his moral code had lost the battle, willingly and completely, to the monster that the song had unleashed. He'd watched helplessly as he'd murdered Melissa, unable to stop himself even as his soul had screamed in horror. He knew the power of that song, and there was no fucking way he would ever trust himself around Abby or anyone else while that song was playing.

How the hell could she look at him and not see the monster he'd become? Instead, she saw only the man he'd tried and failed to be, and she was willing to risk her own life to prove he was the man she wanted him to be.

Desperation coursing through him, he stared up at the blue sky. "What the hell am I supposed to do?" He couldn't afford to be around her, but he owed her his help in finding a four-year-old boy who was out there somewhere in the grasp of a psychopath. As long as he was alive, innocents were at risk. He owed the world his death, but he couldn't help Abby and her nephew if he were dead. There was no way to die and help her at the same time. Her mention of the song was a brutal reminder of the predator he'd become, making it impossible for him to delude himself that he had a right to be with her, touching her, and accepting her trust.

Abby got out of the SUV.

Jace tensed when he heard her door slam. Instinctively, he reached for the gun he'd shoved in the pocket of his jacket. He turned it toward his chest without removing it from his pocket. If she started to sing to him, he was ending it right there. Right then. Without hesitation. His duty to keep her alive had to trump his duty to help her find her nephew. There was no way he was endangering her.

Abby walked around the vehicle, her footsteps almost silent in the deep moss. He turned his head to watch her approach, every muscle in his body taut. She looked right at him, her green eyes steady on his face as she neared him. He caught his breath, his heart thudding almost painfully. She was so beautiful… No, she was so much more than beautiful. She was light, she was love, she was courage, and she was peace... peace he didn't deserve.

She came to a stop in front of him, searching his face.

His fingers tightened on the gun, pressing the muzzle into his ribs, angling it toward his heart. "Don't sing," he warned her. "Don't do it."

She said nothing. She just stood there, studying him. He felt as though she were peeling aside all his layers and exposing the coarse ugliness of his core. He didn't want her to see it. Despite what she'd been through, there was a beauty and purity to her soul that still glittered with life. He didn't want to be the one to finally wipe it out by tainting her with his rotten core. "I think," he said, forcing out the words, "that it would be best if I went on without you. I'll find Seth and bring him back. You go to my place and hole up. It's safe. I'll meet you there."

"Shut up." She grasped the waistband of his jeans, twisting her fingers in the denim. "Just for one second, shut up."

He ignored her. "You're not safe with me. I have to do what's right and that's—"

She grabbed his shoulders, stood on her tiptoes, and kissed him.

Chapter Seven

JACE FROZE. HER lips were warm and soft, tasting faintly like honey or vanilla, or something sweet. Her mouth was inviting, a sensual temptation that tore through all his safeguards and plunged right to his gut.

He wanted to shove her away from him. He *knew* that was the only responsible choice. He *wanted* to be a man he could respect.

But he was so starved for what she gave him that there was no way for him to resist it. He released the gun, and immediately wrapped his arms around her and dragged her against him. Her body was like heavenly sin when she melted against him. With his shirt tied around his ankle as a makeshift splint, the only thing between them was her thin top. He tunneled his hand through her hair, glorifying in the sensation of the silken strands sliding across his fingers.

She slid her arms behind his neck, holding tight, pulling him toward her, still kissing him, coaxing him to respond, to give her what she wanted from him.

He was completely unable to deny her when his need was pouring through him just as strongly. He angled his head and kissed her back, deeply, intensely, offering her what little value there still was in his soul. He couldn't believe how incredible she tasted, how soft her lips were, and how much heat burned through him from her kiss.

He wanted more. He wanted every part of her. He needed to claim her for his own, to protect and cherish her for all eternity. He'd never held anything so innocent and beautiful in his arms before, and he didn't want to ever release her. She was the light he'd been searching for his entire life, a confirmation that he'd been right to stay alive all these years. He palmed her hips, sliding his hands over the curves of her ass, his cock going rock hard at the feel of her body beneath his hands.

He'd been with women before, but he'd been only partially present, always looking over his shoulder for a threat, or thinking about how to better serve his pack. But in this moment, with Abby in his arms, with her scent wrapped around him, with her body entangled with his, there was no room for anything but her. Everything else simply faded away, until all that was left was how badly he wanted her, and how much he needed to safeguard her.

She made a small noise of pleasure in the back of her throat, a sensual purr that awoke his wolf. It roared to life, howling through him as it greedily absorbed every essence of her. His wolf wasn't violent this time, however. It was pure male, driven by a primal instinct to connect with her as a woman.

Driven by the call of his wolf, Jace tightened his grip on her and deepened the kiss, claiming her on every level of her being, taking over the kiss. His moral code that demanded he keep his distance from her vanished, swept away by the sheer intensity of his need for her, and his lupine instinct to claim her. She didn't resist, melting into him, accepting his need, welcoming his demands. She was utterly open to him, trusting him, offering him whatever he wanted.

Her refusal to protect herself from him incited his need to shield her. The softer she was around him, the fiercer his need to ensure her safety became. He didn't want her to lose that softness, to shun it in favor of the hard shields he lived by. She was too entrancing the way she was, too perfect, too real. She touched a part of him that he'd shut down long ago, a part that wanted to live and breathe so badly he couldn't suppress it now that she'd awakened it.

Her hands moved to his side, and her fingers bumped the gun in his pocket. When the cold steel pressed against his side, reality pierced the bubble she'd woven around him. He was so dangerous he'd had a gun trained on his own ribs, and now he was pouring himself into a kiss with the woman whose life he had destroyed?

Swearing, he broke the kiss, pushing her back from him. "I can't do this," he gasped, his voice raw, his entire body burning with the need to drag her back into his arms. "Don't you understand what I am?" Her cheeks were flushed, her expression so completely kissable that he swore again. "Hell, Abby, I'm not the good guy. I can't be honorable when you look at me like that."

She moved closer to him, and he stiffened, forcing his hands behind his head so he couldn't reach for her. He locked his fingers together, trapping himself as she rested her fingers on his bare chest.

She looked up at him. "I've seen evil," she said. "I've tasted it. You're not it."

"I know I'm not evil," he said, trying to catch his breath as she traced designs on his chest. "But I'm a killer. I'm weak, unable to control my wolf. You're not safe with me."

"I am." She framed his face with her hands, forcing him to look at her. "The song caught you off guard before. You didn't have time to prepare, and you had no emotional connection with my sister. That's why it was able to incite you like that." She smiled, a smile so tender that something twisted inside Jace. "But you know about it now, and you have a connection to me. You won't kill me."

Jace wanted to be the guy she believed in. He'd once thought he was. But he knew better now. He released his hands and clasped hers, pressing a kiss to her fingertips. "Since I was born, I've known my reason for existence was to protect those who needed it."

She nodded. "I can see that."

"I created my own pack of outsiders, because I knew no one else could help them. I was the guy who could save them." He pressed her hand to his heart, as if that would help her understand exactly how deeply he lived his words. "My entire being is focused on protecting others. Every living creature that crosses my path automatically falls under that protection. My connection to them is instant. That's what has enabled me to kill the few wolves that I've had to destroy, because they were predators who could not be cured of their bloodlust, and my job is protection." He'd never tried to explain himself before, but with Abby, he wanted to. He needed to. He needed someone to understand what drove him, so that his legacy would not die with him.

Empathy flickered across Abby's face. "I know," she said. "I could tell the moment I heard your voice on my grandmother's doorstep. That's why I came after you."

"No, don't." He brushed his fingers over her lips, silencing her. "What I'm trying to say is that I don't need to know someone personally to have that connection with them. It's instant and complete. I had it with your sister by virtue of the fact that she was a living creature...and yet *I killed her anyway*." He tightened his grip on her hands. "That song overruled everything that has defined me for my entire life. Protection of innocents is *all* that matters to me, and the song broke that. No matter how much you want to believe in me, you can't do it. I'm too dangerous. Do you understand?"

Abby searched his face for a long moment, not answering. As the silence stretched on, a great yearning awoke inside him, a longing to have her refuse to accept his declaration. But at the same time, the yearning also awakened a rising fear in him that she *would* give him what he wanted. If she believed in him and gave him a chance, he knew he'd take it...and that would endanger her, and so many others. His soul burned for her to believe in me, but his moral code needed her to condemn him.

In the end, she said nothing.

She simply lifted his hand and pressed a kiss to each of his knuckles, kisses so tender and intimate that time seemed to stand still. "You're a good man, Jace."

He watched her lips brush over his skin, every cell in his body screaming to drag her into his arms and claim her lips with his. "That's not always enough," he said softly. "And we both know it." But he was glad she'd said it. It felt good to know that she saw past the blood on his hands to the man he tried to be, to the ethics he believed in so deeply.

"It depends on the situation." She stepped back, and took his hands, squeezing gently. "You know the wolf we ran into at my sister's apartment?"

He thought back to the massive black wolf, and the way it had acted so possessively around Abby. His gaze dropped to her belly, which was once again hidden beneath her shirt. "He's the one who did that, isn't he?"

She nodded. "His name is Lucius Stevens. Now that he has found me, he's going to track me down." Her gaze flickered toward his injured ankle. "He's going to come after me, and we both know that you can't stop him on three legs."

Her words were a slap in the face...but they were also true. He was a liability right now, and his leg was not going to heal overnight, and probably never. He ground his jaw. "I'll—"

"I need you, Jace." She held up her shirt, showing him the scars again. "This is what he did the last time he found me. He's angrier now, and bigger. I can't run again, because I need to find Seth. I *must* face him, and I need your help."

He gritted his jaw, and glanced behind her at the silent, ramshackle cabin she'd driven them to. "You're trying to manipulate me into going into that cabin and putting myself in the hands of some healer I don't know and don't trust."

She grinned. "Did it work?"

He ran his hand through his hair. Every instinct told him to walk away and return to his home, where he was in control, so he could take time to heal. Except this time was different. He had a feeling healing wasn't going to happen, and they didn't have time anyway. "How do you know this healer?"

"He's the one who saved my life when Lucius attacked me before," she said. "I'd be dead without him."

Jace looked past her at the cabin again. He couldn't pick up any indication of life from the building, and that made him wary. He hadn't been able to sense Lucius either. "Shifter?"

"Yes."

His gaze shifted to her. "From Grigori's pack?"

"He used to be."

But he could hear the hesitation in her voice. She wasn't certain where the healer's loyalties currently resided, and she was nervous. But she knew they needed help for his leg and her neck. He rested his hands on her shoulders and opened his senses, searching the woods for any indication of wolf. He could smell pine sap, rich soil, and the myriad scents of woodland creatures, but no shifters.

It felt safe, but he knew that could change in an instant. If he were under a healer's spell, he wouldn't be as alert. She was correct that he needed to heal. Shit. He had no choice, did he? Not if he wanted to fulfill his obligation to her. Turning himself over to a shifter he didn't know was foolish, but she was right about his ankle. If there were a way to heal quickly, he needed to try it…but he needed to control the situation. He paused for a moment, then pulled out his phone. Drake answered on the first ring. "What's up?"

"I need a bodyguard. How soon can you get here?" He quickly gave Drake his location.

"Thirty minutes."

"Make it ten." He hung up and shoved his phone back in his pocket. "We wait."

Chapter Eight

ABBY FISTED HER hands in frustration when Jace leaned back against his SUV and folded his arms over his chest, clearly intending not to enter the cabin until Drake appeared. He looked so dangerous and lethal, a predator at rest who was ready to attack in an instant. The only vulnerability was the way he held his right foot off the ground, not even letting his toes rest against the ground. His body was taut, and she knew that he'd blocked the pain from his mind, creating some sort of physical and mental separation between his crushed ankle and the rest of him. Through his incredible self-discipline, it had become a non-factor for him...as long as he didn't have to put weight on it.

Respect surged through her, a deep admiration for the raw strength that propelled him through every moment of his life. No wonder he'd become alpha of a group of renegades. It was impossible not to admire him on a thousand levels.

He looked past her, scanning the woods as he waited. She could feel the heat prickling off him, as if his wolf was pacing just beneath the surface of his skin, restless to be released. She'd felt it come to life when she'd kissed him. She knew she should have been afraid of the wolf, but she hadn't. It had made her feel safe. In her world, that was a precious gift.

But even as she thought about feeling safe, fear rippled through her. She didn't like sitting here, waiting, vulnerable, with Jace injured and a silver bullet her only defense.

"What is it?" He took his gaze off the woods and looked directly at her. His dark eyes were intense, boring into her as if he were trying to see inside her soul.

She shrugged. "I don't like waiting. Grigori and Lucius might guess I would come here. The longer we wait, the more chance they have to find us." She swallowed at the thought of Lucius finding her. Showing Jace her scars had been difficult for her, because it had made her past real again. It had made her remember exactly how terrifying it had been to have Lucius coming after her, that moment of terror when she'd realized she had no way to save herself.

And now he'd found her again.

"I'm paying attention. I'll know if anyone approaches. I've asked the animals to alert me. Even if I don't pick it up, they will." Jace was still watching her carefully, giving her his full attention.

She took a deep breath, trying to calm down, uncomfortable with his penetrating gaze. She didn't want him to see her weakness and fear. She needed to be strong and courageous, because if she let the fear take over, it would debilitate her. "They're very good. They're experts at staying undetected." She couldn't keep from looking around, wondering if there were wolves lurking in the shadows.

Jace studied her. "How did you stop Lucius from killing you?" He kept his voice casual, obviously trying to distract her from their surroundings and her own thoughts. She was relieved Jace had accepted the need to be healed, but that didn't make her any more comfortable with being here.

She shrugged, shifting restlessly. Fear prickled down her spine, and her lungs began to constrict as her mind went back to the attack. "I don't know. He just stopped. I've thought about it hundreds of times, and I still don't have an answer." She restlessly brushed her hair back from her face, trying to stave off the panic attack starting to amass inside her. Standing out in the open, with Lucius potentially on his way to that very spot, was taking its toll on her emotional reserves, wrapping her up in an insidious web of escalating fear.

She felt so vulnerable standing out in the open, even with Jace beside her. She tried to shake out her shoulders, but her hands were starting to tremble. "I think he had a plan that I don't know about." She looked at Jace. "You met him. He's dangerous. He's strong. And right now, he's out there somewhere, planning something..." She looked around. "He could be minutes from here right now. Can we please go inside?"

"No one is approaching. I promise you." Jace held out his hand to her. "Come here," he said softly.

She didn't hesitate. She instinctively set her hand in his, needing the grounding of his touch.

He closed his fingers around hers and tugged gently, drawing her closer. She was too tense to accept, but he increased his pressure. "Come." He gave her hand a sharp tug, knocking her off balance so she fell into him.

The moment her body hit his, he wrapped his arms around her, locking her against him. As soon as she felt his arms encircle her in a protective shield, all her bravado deserted her. She started to shake violently as memories of that horrible night flooded back. Silent tears trailed over her cheeks as she buried her face in Jace's chest, fighting against the panic that had haunted her for so long. Her throat clogged up, and the scars on her stomach burned with agony, as if the wounds were fresh and raw once again. Her breath came in ragged gasps, and her legs began to tremble, as the panic sucked her into its grasp.

"Hey, hey," Jace tightened his arms around her, his lips brushing against her ear. "You're safe now, Abby. I've got you. Do you understand?"

She squeezed her eyes shut, concentrating on the feel of his body against hers. She focused on his scent, a woodsy scent of soap and spice. She fought to ground herself in him, but she couldn't. Flashes of that night kept slashing through her memories, fighting for attention. "I was asleep," she whispered, unable to hold it in. "My apartment was on the tenth floor. I lived in a secured building. I thought I was safe. I knew I was safe. I—" She pulled back to look at Jace. "I woke up when he was dragging me out of my bed by my hair. I tried to scream, but he'd already gagged me."

Something dark flickered in Jace's eyes. "Bastard."

She tried to pace away from him, but his grip tightened on her, keeping her against him. "Talk to me," he said gently, the softness of his voice a vast departure from the anger flashing in his eyes. "What happened?"

"He ripped off my clothes. I thought he was going to try to rape me, but he didn't. He just stripped me and then tied my wrists over my head and attached them to the chandelier in my dining room." She'd never forget how terrified she'd been, how vulnerable, how defenseless. "He said I had to learn who was in charge of me. He...he shifted and then he approached. He licked my stomach and then..." Nausea churned through her. "He bit me. Again, and again. I screamed, and no one heard me. No one stopped him. It felt like hours, and then, suddenly, he left. He just jumped out my window and left me dangling by my wrists. I thought I was going to die, Jace. I was so scared. I still don't sleep at night. Every time I close my eyes, I see him. I hear his howl at night. And then, and then he was there again today. He's back." She swallowed, fighting against the fear trying to grip her. "He's back, Jace."

"I know he is. But this time, you have me."

"He almost killed you already! He's so dangerous. Worse than Grigori—"

"Hey." Jace touched her jaw, forcing her gaze to his. "Look at me. You're safe now. Do you understand? He doesn't have you."

"But he's out there. He's hunting me. He—"

"He will die if he comes near you." The edge to Jace's voice made chills race down her spine. In that moment, she suddenly saw the ruthless alpha who would do whatever it took to protect those who mattered. Gone was the guilt over her sister's death. Gone was his fear about being coerced into a murderous shift. He was elemental alpha, a deadly predator who could never be stopped.

Her heart skipped a beat, and she stared at him, shocked by the change in him. Suddenly, his shattered ankle didn't matter. Nothing could stop him from protecting her. *Nothing.* The fear that had been haunting her for so long slipped away, replaced by a visceral awareness of Jace as a man.

He threaded his fingers through her hair, and lightly tugged her toward him. She went willingly, riveted by the depth of power coursing through him. His lips met hers in an instinctual connection. Her entire body shuddered at the feel of his mouth on hers, at the sensation of his body against hers. He embodied such strength, such honor, such power, and he poured them all into her with his kiss.

His mouth was hot and demanding, but at the same time, there was a gentleness to it that wrapped around her like a shield, protecting her from the darkness of her memories and the haunting whispers of her past. It was the perfect combination of fierceness and tenderness, a seduction that reached inside her and cradled the fragile part of her that was barely holding itself together in the wake of her life.

She melted into him, yielding to his kiss, needing his touch in a way that she'd never needed anyone's. After the incident with Lucius, she'd been wary, afraid to trust, afraid to let anyone get too close, especially men, and, more specifically, shifters. But from that first moment she'd heard Jace's voice, something inside her had reached for him, somehow knowing that he was the secret to her healing.

He growled low in his throat, and angled the kiss, deepening it, asking for more, demanding more, and offering more. She slid her arms around his neck, lacing her fingers together as she leaned into him. Her stomach was against his, the first body that had touched her scars since she'd gotten them. A wolf shifter should trigger the fears that fermented inside her, but Jace's heated strength relaxed her, taking away the tension, giving her the first respite she'd had in so long.

His fingers were light against the back of her neck, caressing her skin, as his other arm locked around her lower back, holding her tight against him, offering her both tenderness and strength. She sighed, turning herself over to his kiss. His kiss was relentless, claiming her with a fierceness that made her belly tighten. He was pure male, and she knew he was staking his claim on her...and she wanted him to.

He broke the kiss and trailed his mouth down the side of her neck, tugging on her hair to tip her head back. Gripping his shoulders, she leaned back, breathing in the chills that raced over her body as he kissed along her neck, her collarbone, and then across her chest. Despite the injury to her neck, she felt no pain, either because he was careful to avoid the injuries, or because his touch eased her pain. His kisses were searing heat, promises of seduction, statements of ownership.

Desire swirled through her, dancing across her heart like flashes of lightning during a summer storm, spinning tighter and tighter, until she felt like she was going to snap. His hands went to her hips, spanning her butt, his fingers digging into the soft flesh as he anchored her against him.

She could feel his erection against her belly, and her body responded with fiery heat, dragging her mercilessly into the spell he was weaving around them. He wasn't simply her protector. He was honor, strength, tenderness, and humanity. As strong as he was, she'd seen the anguish in his eyes. She knew parts of him were broken, utterly shattered, but somehow, someway, he had come alive for her.

"Hey," he pulled back, searching her face as he

brushed his thumb over her cheeks. "No tears," he said softly. "It'll be okay."

"I was crying?" She brushed the back of her hand over her cheek, surprised to find it was damp. "Sorry, I just..." She hesitated, unsure whether to say it. On some levels, she didn't know Jace at all, but at the same time, she felt as if she saw into his heart in a way no one else did, and that she gave him something he needed.

His dark gaze was steady, unflinching, as he continued to stroke her cheek. "You just what?"

She swallowed, something about his unyielding gaze reaching deep inside her and making her want to connect. "You make me feel safe and treasured," she told him. "I never thought I could feel like that." Her cheeks flushed. "It feels amazing to have you touch me the way you do. I didn't think I'd ever want another man's hands on my body, but somehow, it's different with you." Heat flushed her face when he said nothing, and suddenly she felt stupid for being so open. "Nevermind. Forget it. I—"

"No." He caught her jaw with his hand as she tried to turn away. His eyes were haunted. "I feel it too," he said softly. "I've been living in hell since I killed Melissa. I can't think. I can't focus. I can't see anything but darkness. But when I'm with you, I have these flashes where I can think again, where I feel like there might be a reason why I'm still supposed to be alive." His eyes glittered. "Thank you," he said softly.

Her heart flipped at the depth of emotion in his voice. Somehow, in the midst of their insane worlds, something had connected them. Death, guilt, pain, fear? Horrible things that had somehow dragged them both into the sunshine long enough to breathe again.

She nodded. "Don't kill yourself. I need you."

The corner of his mouth tilted up, the first hint of a real smile she'd ever seen from him. "I am beginning to see that."

She smiled too, her body beginning to relax. His arms were still around her, his fingers drawing circles on her hips, through her jeans. Her body was still humming with desire, but at the same time, there was something else. A sense of peace. Of safety. Of knowing that she was in the right place at this moment.

His gaze went to her mouth, and her pulse quickened.

Tension sprang between them. It was an unstoppable hunger, an untamed need to continue what they'd started. She held her breath, her fingers tightening on his shoulders as his palms pressed more heavily against her hips.

"I don't have the right to even consider kissing you," he said, even as he pulled her closer. "I fucked up everything for you."

"No." She put her hands on his chest, stopping him. Anger rushed through her. "Don't you understand, Jace? It's not your fault. Grigori and Lucius were going to take Seth from my sister, no matter what. If it hadn't worked with you, it would have happened anyway." Tears filled her eyes, but she blinked them away. "She ran away with Grigori's grandson. Do you honestly think they would have allowed her to live?"

Denial flashed in his eyes. "If I had resisted that song—'

"You couldn't have! It's too strong! Don't you get it?"

He narrowed his eyes. "You said you could desensitize me to the song. Which is it, Abby? Is the song so powerful that no wolf alive could resist its call? Or is it beatable, and I simply failed?"

"No one can break it without the right training. It's impossible. But with the right training, it's possible for some wolves." She met his gaze. "If you noticed, Damien was there when my sister was killed, and he didn't shift. Grigori was there, and he didn't shift either."

Jace's expression was stunned at her words. He dropped his hands as if she'd burned him. "Son of a bitch," he said, his voice raw. "I didn't even think of that. They didn't shift. Only me. I'm the fucking alpha, and I was the one who didn't have enough control. *Fuck!*" He pushed her back and then held his hands up. His face was stricken, and she realized that in her attempt to encourage him, she'd given him the fuel to condemn himself the final time.

"Jace, no! They had training—"

"Damien was weak and pathetic," he snapped. "*Weak.* And yet, he didn't shift." He stepped away from her, but the moment he set his right foot down, he collapsed, dropping to the ground as his body literally gave out from the onslaught of pain that had burst through his shield.

Abby lunged for him, but he was too heavy, and she fell with him, tumbling to the ground beside him. They had just hit the ground when she heard the front door of the cabin open.

Jace swore, and rolled to his side, stumbling back to his feet, his body shaking as he scrambled to get back up.

But it was too late.

A black shadow streaked out the front door and launched itself at him.

Chapter Nine

JACE BRACED HIMSELF a split second before he was hit squarely in the chest by a scrawny black wolf that hit him with surprising, desperate force. He grabbed his assailant and flung her into the car, spinning himself out of the way as he did so. He leapt over to Abby and landed in front of her on one foot, crouching and ready. Pain flooded his body, but he shut it down, every last bit of his energy focused on protecting her.

The black wolf that had attacked him landed easily on all four feet, her upper lip raised in a snarl as she whirled back toward them.

Jace went still, holding back his own wolf, while he watched the female. She was lean and wiry, as if she'd lived a life skulking through alleys foraging for food, always prepared to fend off assailants. She was a wolf of the streets, the most dangerous and unpredictable kind in existence, because she lived by no rules. "I'm not here to hurt you," he said, attuning his senses to the cabin behind them, checking for the presence of any more wolves. He didn't like having his back to the cabin, so he pressed back against Abby, shifting her to the side so he could get them in a better position.

Abby was right behind him, her body rigid with fear. "Where's Kiernan?" He could smell her fear, but her voice was steady and strong.

The black wolf looked back and forth between them, her lips still raised in a silent snarl.

"We're here to see Kiernan," Abby repeated. "Where is he?"

The black wolf didn't move, her body taut as she watched them. Everything about her spoke of aggression, and a willingness to fight to the death. Jace's wolf fought to emerge, preparing for a battle, but he shoved it aside. He would not attack a female. There was no fucking way he was going to hurt another woman again. *Ever.* "Stand down," he snapped. "We're here in peace!"

I got her. Drake's voice drifted through his mind. *Keep her distracted.*

Jace couldn't smell Drake, and he knew his teammate was approaching downwind. Jace crouched lower, letting his wolf pace closer to the surface, letting the female shifter know that he was her equal. *Don't hurt her, Drake.*

She gets mercy only if she deserves it. Drake's voice was cool, without emotion, the voice of a soldier prepared to do whatever he needed. Jace swore, not liking the tone of Drake's voice. When had Drake begun to lose his humanity?

Abby touched his shoulder. "Don't shift," she said softly. "It's not safe."

Something about the edge to her voice caught his

attention, and he stiffened. "Why not?"

"The song. I can hear it in your blood right now. If you shift again, it might own you."

He went cold, and fury coursed through him. What else did she know about that song? What had she not told him? "Abby—" The female wolf shifted position, drawing his attention back to her.

She'd focused on his injured leg, and he felt her sudden surge of energy. Son of a bitch. She was going to attack him and try to take advantage of his injury. "Stand down," he said again, using the voice he'd perfected with his fucked up pack when they were losing their shit.

She tensed her body, and then sprang at them, clearly immune to his fantastic powers of persuasion.

Jace swore, throwing himself in front of Abby as he held up his arm to block their assailant. The black wolf's teeth sank into his forearm, tearing flesh he couldn't afford to lose. With his leg injury, he couldn't get the leverage to defeat her without shifting, and his wolf knew it. It howled with the need to be released, but Jace fought it back with iron control. Even without Abby's warning, he would have known he couldn't shift. He was too close to the edge of control, and if his wolf took over, it would own him.

It would be a lethal killer he couldn't control. He'd rather have his throat ripped out than unleash himself onto the world, or this wolf.

There was something about the female that made the song hum even more loudly through his veins, calling to the monster Grigori had unleashed. He couldn't shift to his wolf form, but he knew he would lose if he didn't. Die or kill? Those were shitty options even for a guy with his morals. He wouldn't kill the she-wolf, but he wouldn't risk Abby either by letting himself get killed.

"Get to the car," he ordered Abby as he slammed his elbow into the wolf's ribs, trying to dislodge her teeth from his arm. She didn't let go, her teeth grinding deeper into his arm. "Get out of here!"

Abby didn't move. "No, I can't leave you—"

"Go!" He shoved her backward as the wolf tore at his arm. She threw him off balance, and he had to put his right foot down to keep from falling. The pain ripped through him, and his leg collapsed—

A silver wolf charged out of the woods. Drake tore across the grass and leapt on the black wolf, his teeth sinking into the back of her neck. She released Jace and whirled around, trying to dislodge Drake, but she had no chance. He was too heavy, and he'd gotten a perfect grip on her, because she'd been too focused on crushing Jace's forearm instead of paying attention to her surroundings.

It was a rookie mistake, an unusual lapse in judgement that he wouldn't have expected from a savvy street wolf. She should have been accustomed to always focusing on all possible threats, but she hadn't. It was an anomaly he'd contemplate when he wasn't in so much fucking pain.

Swearing, Jace rolled to his side, fighting against the nausea. He was an expert at shutting down pain, but between his ankle and his arm, it was impossible to keep it all at bay. Jesus. Pain was inconvenient as hell.

Abby crouched beside him, still too close to danger. "Let me help you up," she said urgently, her gaze flicking to the battle between Drake and the alley wolf.

"Get back," he gritted out. "Now."

"No. We have to get inside. We have to find

Kiernan." She grabbed his uninjured arm, helping him up. He staggered, trying to keep his balance on one leg. His arm was torn, the ligaments and muscles heavily damaged. He'd almost been taken out by a street wolf half his size, a wolf he could usually take down without even an extra breath. What the hell? Even injured he shouldn't have been hit so hard. His timing had been slow, his awareness compromised, things that should have nothing to do with his injured leg.

Grigori had stolen everything from him: his values, his leg, and his freedom to shift. He was fucking defenseless, at a time when he needed to be the strongest he'd ever been.

"Come on!" Abby tugged at him. "We need to get inside. Something's wrong!"

He knew he had no choice. He'd been pushed to the limit physically. If there was any chance of being healed, he had to take it. If he didn't, he was a liability, and he would not be able to keep her safe, rescue the kid, or somehow fix the hell he'd brought down upon them. "Let's go." He put his hand on her back, urging her forward as he followed her, keeping one eye on Drake, who had the female pinned to the earth, using his teeth and his massive bodyweight to hold her still.

She was snarling, her ears pinned flat, waiting for a chance to take him. Jace could feel the energy rippling through her, building like a volcano preparing to erupt. "Careful with her, Drake."

Drake growled and tightened his grip on her neck, every muscle taut. Jace knew that Drake sensed exactly how dangerous she was, and he was ready.

"Hold her," Jace commanded, just as Abby spun away from him, yanked open the door to the cabin and ducked inside. "Hey. Wait!" He hopped after her, gritting his teeth as she disappeared out of sight into the darkened building.

He grabbed his gun out of his waistband and cocked it, holding it ready as he eased inside the shadowed cabin. A silver bullet could never be dispensed without great necessity and forethought due to how deadly it was, and Jace had never actually fired a silver bullet into anything, but right now, he was as close to that edge as he'd ever been.

He crossed the threshold. The door swung shut behind him, plunging him into darkness.

Chapter Ten

H E WENT STILL, his back up against the door as he waited for his eyes to adjust. "Abby," he said softly. "Tell me where you are. I don't want to shoot you."

"To your right."

At the sound of her voice, he immediately honed in on her location. He leapt across the room, landing beside her, keeping all his weight on his strong leg. She jumped, but he grabbed her arm, pulling her against him. "Where's the light?"

"It's out. There's a door at the back. We need to go there."

He moved first, hopping across the floor. He reached the door and then readied his weapon. Outside, the sounds of the scuffle had stopped, and the inside of the cabin was eerily silent. He was aware of Abby right behind him, and then he slowly tested the doorknob.

It turned easily, and he shoved at the door. It creaked open, and he went still, ready, his senses on alert for any movement.

There was nothing, but he caught the strong scent

of male wolf, pungent and thick. He leapt into the room, landing on one foot, ready.

Stretched out on a narrow bed was a man, heavily bandaged, breathing shallowly. He was wearing only jeans, his bare torso wrapped tightly, though blood was still leaking through the bandages. It was a wolf, a shifter who'd been brutally attacked. The wolf needed protection, and suddenly he understood the ferocity of the female's attack outside. "Kiernan?" he asked Abby.

"No." She looked around the room, searching just as he was.

There were no other beds. No other occupants. Just the one man on the edge of death.

Jace pointed the gun toward the closet. "Open it and step back."

Abby hurried over to the door. She grabbed the doorknob and leapt back as she pulled it open. Nothing leapt out, and an assortment of men's clothing was hanging in haphazard fashion from the rack. Jace eased over to it, opening all his senses. He could smell wolf, but it wasn't the same scent as the man in the bed. "Kiernan's things, I assume." He nudged the clothes aside, but there was no trap door to another room, and no healer hiding among the garments. "Not here."

He turned around and faced the room again. There were no other doors, and the windows looked out into the woods. There were no more rooms in the cabin. That was it. "He's not here." Disappointment flooded him, and, belatedly, he realized that he'd been holding out hope that this healer could work his magic on him, and somehow fix his shattered leg.

Abby met his gaze, and fear flickered across her face. Her fingers brushed against the wound on her neck, and he swore, all too aware that his injuries weren't the only ones at risk. "Would Kiernan have been able to decrease the amount of wolf protein in your blood from the bite?"

She nodded. "That's what he did last time. I think that's why it didn't turn me."

Jace ground his jaw, looking around the small room. "So, what do we do now?"

"There's another room."

Jace glanced sharply at Abby. "What?"

"I was here for months being healed, but I wasn't in either of these rooms." She walked along the wall, trailing her hands over the plaster, her brow furrowed. "I was unconscious when I was brought here. In addition, on the day I went home, I woke up in this room in the morning, but when I was healing, I wasn't in these rooms." She looked at him. "There's somewhere else he does his work."

Jace ran his hand through his hair. "That could be anywhere—"

"No, it couldn't." She looked up at the ceiling. "There were times I could hear him talking to other people. I could hear what was going on in here. It's somewhere close."

Jace frowned and looked around again. He'd seen the outside of the cabin and he knew the perimeter was accounted for, and it was clear there was no second story. "There's only one option. It has to be underneath." He grabbed a bandage from a stash by the bed and wrapped it around his arm, using his teeth to secure it. As he wrapped it, he studied the floor carefully, inspecting each of the boards. Abby did the same, carefully testing each one, in the closet and in the main area.

After they'd both checked the entire floor, she

looked at him. "Nothing?"

"Nothing."

The shifter in the bed groaned, and Jace glanced over at him. He was surprised to see his eyes open and watching them. His mouth moved, as if he was trying to say something, fighting for consciousness.

The same instincts that had turned him into an alpha willing to protect his wolves made him go to the injured wolf and crouch next to him. "What is it?"

The shifter's eyes were bloodshot. "My sister," he croaked. "Help her."

"Your sister?"

"That must be the black wolf Drake has," Abby gasped. "Oh, God, she was trying to keep her brother safe, not attack us offensively. I need to go get her—"

Jace locked his fingers around her wrist, keeping her close. There was no chance he was sending her out there until he had more information. "What happened to you?" As he asked, he scanned the shifter, cataloguing his injuries. Most of the damage appeared to have been centered on his abdomen...much like Abby's. "Lucius?"

The shifter closed his eyes and nodded. Abby tensed, her fingers digging into Jace's shoulder. "Lucius did this?" she whispered. "It's the same as what he did to me." She looked over her shoulder at the window. "We need to get out of here."

Jace put his hand on the shifter's forehead. His skin was cold, too cold. Shifters always ran hot, even when they weren't about to shift. The man was in dangerous condition, which was probably why his sister had brought him to Kiernan...only Kiernan couldn't be found. He leaned forward, sensing what the shifter needed from him. "I'll make sure your sister is safe from him."

The shifter nodded once, almost imperceptibly, but the tension slipped from his body, as if he were finally letting go.

"Oh, no." Abby fell to her knees beside him. "No, don't give up. We'll find Kiernan. He'll save you."

The shifter didn't respond. His only movement was the very shallow movement of his chest as he breathed.

"No! Don't give up!" Abby grabbed his hand, pressing it between her palms, tears pooling in her eyes. "Come on! Don't let him win."

Jace set his hand on her back, rubbing gently, even though he knew he couldn't take away the pain of her memories, and the moment. "We need to get his sister, so she can say goodbye."

Abby looked up at him, tears glistening in her eyes. "Lucius has killed so many," she whispered. "I can't do this anymore."

"You can. Seth needs us." Jace grabbed the edge of the bed and hauled himself up. "We need to get this guy's sister—"

Abby leapt up. "I'll do it. She won't trust you or Drake. You stay here with him."

"I'm not leaving you—"

"Drake is outside!" she shouted at him, suddenly angry. "Someone needs to stay with him. It has to be you."

Jace frowned. "Me? Why?"

"Because you're a wolf! Don't you get it?"

Jace caught her arm, holding gently. "No," he said softly. "I don't get it. Talk to me."

"My sister died alone! I was alone in that room for almost twenty-four hours after Lucius attacked me. My mom was killed and left to die alone." Tears glistened on her cheeks, and her hands started to shake. "Do you know what it's like to think you're going to die alone? That no one else understands the pain you're in? That there are so many things left undone and you can't do them, because there's no one coming to help? Because no one is going to come in time? Don't you get it?"

Her pain was raw and ragged, spilling out from the place he knew she'd kept it locked up for so long. Silently, he wrapped his good arm around her and pulled her against him. For a split second, she fought it, and then she collapsed into him, burying her face in his shoulder.

Jace pressed a kiss to her hair. "I won't let that happen to you," he said quietly. "I will track you down no matter what happens. I swear it." As he said the words, he realized he meant it. Not for Seth's sake. Not to atone for the fact he'd killed her sister. But simply because of her, because she mattered. Yeah, he knew he would never be worthy of her after what he'd done, but that didn't change the fact that her bravery and loyalty affected him deeply. Those traits were the core of what defined him and so few people lived by them. But she did.

He ached for the pain she'd endured, for the fear she'd lived under for so long. He had to make it end. He had to give her the freedom to live without fear again. Suddenly, it wasn't simply about rescuing Seth. It was about giving the woman in his arms the ability to live again without the memories haunting her.

Abby pulled back, searching his face. "Say it again."

"Which part? That I won't let it happen to you?" At her nod, he tightened his grip on her, pulling her tight against him. "I won't let that piece of shit ever touch you again," he said. "I will track you down and find you, no matter what happens. I give you my oath."

She searched his face, and sudden tears glistened in her eyes. "I'll hold you to that, Jace," her voice was thick with emotion, tainted with the fear that had haunted her since Lucius's attack.

"You won't need to. I meant it. I keep my promises." How the hell he was going to do it with half his limbs compromised, he didn't know, but it didn't matter. There was something about Abby that awakened his protective instincts. She wasn't a stray wolf who needed containment. She was love, courage, and loyalty, things that were so lost in the world he lived in. Somehow, he felt as though his job was to be her strength, to create the safe place for her that would allow her light to continue to shine. "Stay here." He wrapped his arm around her and reached out for Drake. *The alley wolf's brother is in here dying. She was protecting him. Let her in. He doesn't have much time.*

There was a pulse of respect from Drake. *Got it.*

Jace's good leg was aching now, and his muscles were beginning to tremble from the effort of supporting himself. As his adrenaline began to fade, the extent of his injuries became more apparent. The bandages on his arm were already soaked with blood, as were those on his ankle. He'd lost far too much blood already, and his body had little healing strength remaining.

"Jace?" Abby frowned, and suddenly he realized his legs were giving out on him. He tried to right himself, but the ground seemed to rise up and grab him. Abby grabbed for him, but her fingers slipped off as he hit the ground.

He rolled onto his back, the gun across his chest as Abby crouched beside him. "Jace!"

"I just need a second."

He heard the front door open, and he gestured at Abby. "Get back. I need a clear line to the door."

"You're going to shoot her?"

"If I have to." His vision swam out of focus, but he rolled onto his side and raised his gun, leveling it at the door. He was innately aware of Abby behind him, and he knew exactly where she was. The door opened, and Jace tensed.

Drake's silver wolf walked in first, blocking the door as he scanned the room. He saw Jace on the floor, and his eyes narrowed. He immediately trotted over to Jace and stood beside him, facing the door, offering his alpha his protection. *This is stupid, Jace. You don't know what she's capable of.*

Her brother's dying. It was enough.

The alley wolf appeared in the door, crouched low, her lips curled in a snarl as she eyed the room, prepared for a trap, just as Jace was. Jace kept the gun on her. "I will use this," he said. "Don't make me. I promised your brother I would keep you safe from Lucius. You're under my protection now."

At the mention of her brother, she snapped her gaze to the cot. When she saw how still he was, she let out a low whine and sprinted across the room. She nudged him, whining softly, her tail tucked between her legs. With a soft cry of distress, she shifted back to human form, taking her brother's hand in hers. "Roarke, you have to hang on. Don't give up." Tears rolled down her cheeks, and Jace felt the urge to look away, to give her privacy, but he couldn't take the risk.

Drake shifted to human form with innate ease, grabbed a sheet off a stack in the corner, and then strode across the room. The woman leapt up, her eyes wide with fear as he approached. He held out the sheet silently. She glanced down, belatedly realizing her nakedness, and took the sheet from him with a quick nod of appreciation.

Drake stepped back as she wrapped it around herself and sank down on her brother's cot, holding his hand between hers.

Jace groaned and lowered the gun, rolling onto his back again. "Put some clothes on," he gritted out. He hadn't even noticed the woman's nudity, but he was extremely aware that Drake was parading around in front of Abby stark naked. He was surprised to realize he didn't like it. It was his wolf reacting, claiming Abby as his own.

Drake raised his brows, glanced at Abby, who cleared her throat and looked away. He winked at Jace, and then strolled to the closet. "On it."

"We need to find the other room." Jace rolled to his side, grunting with pain when his arm bumped the floor.

"What other room?" Drake asked as he grabbed a pair of jeans from the closet. He was watching the brother and sister duo carefully, not taking his gaze off them.

"I don't know." Jace glanced at Abby. She understood his unspoken need, and crouched beside him to help him to his feet. He swayed against her, fighting to keep his balance. "This place belongs to a powerful healer. There's a hidden room somewhere. We need to find it."

Drake narrowed his eyes, watching Jace carefully. "What happened to you?"

"Bear trap. Wolf bite. A few minor injuries." Jace closed his eyes, reaching out with his senses. There were no other wolves around, but he reached past the superficial information in the air, summoning the depth of his powers that had propelled him to an alpha position. He latched onto Kiernan's scent, allowing it to reach inside him. He softened his mind, allowing his essence to mingle with the molecules in the air, becoming one with them, so he could pick up every nuance in the cabin. It was risky to do it, because he lost contact with his present, but he knew Drake had his back, and they were in trouble.

His mind flew through the room, searching every corner, every nook, every sliver, for the scent he knew had to exist. He tunneled through the room they were in, and then out into the main room. He felt his way along the boards, but again, there was nothing. No trail at all. Swearing, he retraced his steps, back to their room, to the closet where the scent was the strongest... Stronger than it should have been. "It's in the closet."

He opened his eyes, surprised to find he was on the ground again, with Abby's cool hands on his forehead. Her touch felt amazing, easing the heat boiling within him. Her brow was furrowed. "You passed out."

"I did not." He tried to sit up, swaying toward her in a ridiculous display of weakness. "I was focusing." Drake held out his hand, and Jace grabbed it, allowing the other wolf to pull him to his feet. He was showing his weakness now, an often fatal move for an alpha, but he didn't care anymore.

Too much was at stake. He trusted Drake to stand by him, and protect him. "The closet."

Leaning on Abby, he headed toward the closet again, feeling the walls of it again. Abby helped him, her body brushing up against his as they went over each inch of the closet.

"Jace! Look! Here!"

He leaned over her, his shoulder brushing hers as he pressed his fingers to a divot in the wood. The wood was smooth and polished, as if it had been worn smooth by years of touching. "This has to be it." He moved his fingers over the crevice, trying to figure out how to open it.

"Jace." Drake's voice was taut. "Wolves incoming. At least ten. From the north."

Jace spun around and lifted his head, reaching out, but he couldn't pick anything up. No scent. No sound. But Drake didn't need scent or sound. He could sense wolves from miles away, based only on their energy signature. "Grigori?"

Abby sucked in her breath and swung around, her fingers digging into Jace's shoulder. "Lucius?"

"Not Grigori, but they're not hiding their approach. They're moving fast." Drake was standing in the middle of the room, staring at the north wall as if he could see right through it. "They're in vehicles. Moving fast."

"Oh, God." The girl by the bed leapt to her feet. "They followed us. Oh, no." She spun around, her eyes wild. "We have to leave," she said. "They'll kill us—"

"No time. They're too close." Drake met Jace's gaze. No words were spoken, but he knew the stakes. There was no way they would win, not with Jace's injuries, against ten wolves trained by Grigori.

Swearing, he ran his fingers over the wall of the closet. "We need to open this and get in there."

Abby flung herself at the wall, frantically searching. "It has to be somewhere. A hinge or something."

Drake strode over to the bed. "I'll get your brother. Help them search."

For a split second, the woman stared at Drake. Jace

understood her dilemma. How could she trust strangers? But how could she not? They were all the chance she and her brother had. Finally, she nodded. "If you hurt him, I will kill you," she snapped.

"You can try," Drake said mildly, even as he reached past her to pick up her brother.

Clutching the sheet around her, she raced over to the closet, dropping to her knees beside Abby, frantically running her hands over the back wall of the closet, looking for a trigger point that would open some hidden door

Drake moved up behind them, the injured shifter in his arms. "Three minutes until arrival."

Jace swore and thudded his fist against the wood. This wasn't working. They didn't have time to search randomly. He needed a strategy, and he needed it now. "Abby."

She whirled around to look at him, her face ashen. "It's Lucius," she whispered. "I know it's him. He's coming."

Her fear stuck him like a cold knife, and he swore at his answering instinct to drag her into his arms, sprint to the car and get her to safety. Except there was only one road out, and they'd run into the incoming shifters on their way. Their only option was to open the blasted door.

Jace set his hands on her shoulders, gazing steadily at her face, as if the clock wasn't ticking with deadly quickness. "Abby. You know Kiernan well. What would he use as a safeguard to protect his entrance?"

She looked at him frantically. "Seriously? I don't know—"

"You do know." He tightened his grip on her shoulders. "Close your eyes and picture him. He must have come and gone countless times while you were his patient. You *must* know how he does it."

"Two minutes," Drake said.

Jace ignored him, forced himself to remain calm, sending out reassuring energy to Abby. "You've got this, Abby. I know you do."

She glanced at the others, and then back at him. Her face was ashen. "Jace—"

"You can do this."

If she couldn't, they were all dead.

Chapter Eleven

Panic HAMMERED AT Abby, but she focused her attention on Jace. His gaze was steady, his jaw flexed. He acted as if they had all the time in the world, and that took a little bit of the edge off her.

"Come on!" The female shifter banged her fist on the back of the closet, anguish tearing through her voice. Her fear knifed through Abby, jerking her back to awareness. This wasn't just about her. It was about all of them, including another woman who was on Lucius's radar.

It was up to her. Fierce determination surged through her. She squeezed her eyes shut and let her thoughts race back to the hellish recovery time she'd tried so hard to forget. She remembered the scents of earth and healing. Of plants. She remembered the pain—

"It's okay." Jace lightly squeezed her shoulders, his voice forming a protective shield around the memories, giving her the distance she needed to focus on it.

"You're safe."

She wrapped her fingers around Jace's wrists, grounding herself in his solid strength as she tumbled back into the past. Her mind flashed around the room she'd been confined to for so long. She ignored the things that weren't relevant, her thoughts racing to the door at the end of the room, the one where Kiernan always emerged from.

She thought back to the sounds that had always indicated his arrival. The sound of a gentle wind, the light scratching of a bird searching for earthworms, the whisper-light sound of his footsteps. Kiernan was grace and beauty. Understated. Light, like a feather, moving through life with more delicacy than anyone she'd ever met——

Her eyes snapped open. "I know."

"What is it?"

"Finesse." She raced to the back of the closet, where the polished wood was. She bent forward so her lips were hovering above it. Lightly, so lightly, she blew on it, the faintest breath of wind. As her breath warmed the wood, she lightly scratched the worn wood, letting her fingernails drift over it so softly that it would never leave a mark.

For a brief moment, nothing happened.

Something thudded against the front door. Lucius?

She did it again, breathing and scratching. And then a third time—

The back of the closet slid to the side, opening to a pitch-black stairway.

"Go!" Jace whispered.

"I have to close it. You first."

Jace gestured for Drake and the female wolf. They raced through, hurtling down the stairs. Jace shut the exterior closet door, then grabbed Abby. They raced through the hidden door together. The front door of the cabin crashed open and she whirled around, frantically running her hands over the wood to find the smooth spot on the inside of the door to close it. With the closet door shut, it was pitch black, too dark to see. "I can't find it!"

"Here!" Jace grabbed her hand, and brought her fingers to a section of smooth wood.

She leaned forward and blew on it, lightly scratching. One.

Toenails scrabbled on the wood, in the front room.

She breathed and scratched again. Two.

The bedroom slammed open.

Three.

The secret door slid shut with silent, well-oiled perfection.

Jace pulled her against his chest as it closed, both of them staring into the closet, waiting for the door to open. The first crack of light shone, and then the slider closed, sealing them in the darkness.

She started to run, but Jace's arm's tightened around her, holding her in place. "Don't move." His lips brushed against her ear, so softly she could barely hear it.

She froze, realizing that any sound would alert Lucius that they were there. He'd smell their scent, but he would see no way through the closet. If he heard them, however, he'd know they were there, and he'd do whatever it took to get through.

She closed her eyes, pressing herself against Jace's chest as she heard the snuffling of a wolf on the other side of the door. He was scenting her, trying to figure out where she was. Fear constricted her chest, and her heart began to hammer frantically. Lucius was only inches away from her. *Inches.* She had to run. She couldn't stay there, just waiting for him to break through the door—

Jace pressed a kiss to the side of her neck, his arms tightening around her. His chest was powerful and warm against her back, his arms heavily muscled as they crossed over her breasts. She had nowhere to go, completely trapped against him. She was his prisoner, but by being confined to his embrace, it meant she wasn't alone.

This deadly, powerful alpha was her protector, and his tight embrace was his reminder that she could count on him, to help her stay silent, to protect her if Lucius broke through, to do whatever it took.

He rested his head against hers, his cheek warm, his whiskers rough.

Abby took a shallow breath, trying to stay quiet as she focused on Jace, instead of the sounds of frantic scratching from the closet, as if Lucius was trying to dig through the floor. She concentrated on Jace's scent, an earthy combination of male and something else, something warmer, something that seemed to ease through her and take the edge off her panic.

He pressed another kiss to her neck, lower this time, almost at her collarbone. The kiss was longer this time, almost as if he were tasting her, or tempting her. Chills rippled down her spine, but they weren't from fear. They were from a sudden awareness of the intimacy of their situation. His forearms were across her breasts, pressing into her nipples. His pelvis was against her bum, nestled intimately. His lips were a shivery whisper along her neck.

A thud from the closet made her jump, but Jace

tightened his arms around her, steadying her.

She closed her eyes, focusing on Jace. She breathed in his woodsy, masculine scent. She concentrated on the heat of his body, on the solidity of his frame as he held her. His arms were tight around her, his breath sending goosebumps down her back as he feathered kisses along her neck and her collarbone.

Desire fluttered in her belly, which was shocking given their situation, but she didn't fight it. She allowed Jace's presence to fill her completely, breaking through the fear tearing her down, and replacing it with a deep awareness of him as a man, of the energy sparking between them. Suddenly, her muscles didn't feel frozen with terror. Energy poured into her, a searing strength that curled through her, unwrapping every cowering part of her.

There was a thump from the bedroom, but she barely noticed it. Jace had captured her full attention, every nerve primed and waiting for his next touch.

He lightly bit her ear, his arm moving slightly so that his forearm rested against the underside of her breasts. The kisses beside by the car had been intoxicating, but this was different. It was tightly contained desire that couldn't be released. No sounds. No movement. Not even a whisper of response was allowed, with danger so close.

And yet, despite the absolute stillness of their embrace, the desire snaking through her body was fierce and bold, commanding a response from her that she couldn't give.

Jace caught her chin and turned her head toward the side, giving him better access. He kissed along her jaw, butterfly kisses that were so faint that she had to strain to feel them. His lips caressed her skin, moving closer and closer to her lips, until he finally pressed a kiss to the corner of her mouth.

She fought the urge to inhale, to breathe in his presence, to turn in his arms and surrender to the desire he was stoking within her. Her nipples ached at the feel of his arm pressing against them, but when he splayed his other palm low across her belly, pulling her back against him, the intensity of the desire coiling within her became almost too much.

He kissed the corner of her mouth again, a silent, sensual demand. Her heart started to pound, she turned her head further, just enough...

He caught her mouth with his, a searing, claiming kiss that tore through her, making her belly pulse beneath his palm. Her hips moved involuntarily, pressing back against him as he kissed her, his tongue probing, demanding, caressing.

Danger was so close, and yet, with the closet wall between them, they were safe...as long as they were silent. One step down the staircase, and Lucius and his crew would hear them. There was no way she should be kissing Jace right now, no way she should feel safe enough to actually respond. But she knew Jace was aware of every sound from Kiernan's cabin, and he was tracking everything. Jace was simply too lethal to be distracted by a kiss—

He slipped his fingers past the waistband of her jeans, his hand warm on her belly.

She sucked in her breath, but he caught her gasp in a searing kiss, his forearm tightening over her breasts, trapping her against his body. What was he doing? This wasn't the time for this—

He slid his hand lower, his fingertips brushing against the waistband of her underwear. For a split second, she wished that she was the way she'd once been, wearing silk thongs and lacy bras just to feel sexy. Since the attack by Lucius, she'd hid behind cotton underwear and sports bras, refusing to allow herself to crave the touch of a man, unable to even imagine trusting a man enough to let him touch her intimately. But now, with Jace's hand sliding over the cotton, she wished, oh, how she wished, she could be the woman she'd once been, to respond to him the way she wanted to.

But she wasn't.

She was broken. Afraid. Damaged.

Tears burned in her eyes as she caught his wrist, stopping him.

He immediately moved his hand higher, back to her stomach. This time, however, he kept his hand beneath her shirt, so he was still touching her bare skin. He traced circles on her skin, tender, seductive caresses that made her belly tighten...until she realized he was tracing the scars on her stomach.

Revulsion tore through her, and she grabbed his wrist again, trying to get his hand away from her. She didn't want this. She didn't want to be exposed like this. She didn't want to need a man's touch like she needed Jace's. She didn't want to be hiding in the shadows being fondled by one shifter while another hunted her. This wasn't who she wanted to be. She wanted to be outside, in the sunshine, running free, without fear, without constraint.

But Jace didn't let her move his hand. He kept it pressed to her belly, still tracing designs on her skin. She wanted to smack his hand. She wanted to wrench herself out of his arms and shout at him to leave her alone. But she was trapped by the threat of Lucius, unable to make a sound or any kind of movement that would make him aware that they were right on the other side of the wall.

Tears trickling down her cheeks, she leaned her back against Jace's shoulder, unable to run away from him or what he was making her feel. She gave up fighting, and tried to find that place she'd been living in for so long, the one where she shut down everything that made her heart hurt, everything that made her scared, everything that made her feel.

She tried to make herself hard again, but Jace's rhythmic touch on her belly kept distracting her. She squeezed her eyes shut, trying to ignore him, but she couldn't. His hand was warm and steady. It felt as though he were pouring heat into her belly, releasing the knots that had been there for so long. His body was relaxed, not tensed with revulsion at what he was touching. She tried to keep herself tense, preparing for when he'd decide he'd had enough and withdrew the touch that felt so good.

Except, he didn't stop. He didn't try to move his hand lower again. He simply kept his hand on her belly, tracing light circles on her skin. Her skin was so scarred she shouldn't have been able to feel him so well, but somehow, his touch was able to penetrate the deadened nerves. Slowly, ever so slowly, she began to relax into his touch. It began to feel natural to have him touching her damaged body. Comforting. Reassuring.

He pressed a kiss to the side of her neck again, and she closed her eyes, focusing on the sensation of being so close to him. They were touching in so many places. Her back against his chest. His lips on her neck. His forearm across her breasts. His hand on her stomach.

So much physical contact breathing warmth and heat into her. It was surreal and beautiful, something she'd gone without for so long that she'd forgotten how much she needed it.

Or maybe it wasn't simply being touched. Maybe it was *Jace's* touch that felt so good. He made her feel beautiful, not disfigured. He made her feel safe, not afraid. He made her feel alive, like a woman, like someone who wasn't broken irretrievably.

Slowly, hesitantly, almost afraid he wouldn't be there, she turned her head to the side again, tipping her chin back over her shoulder toward him. His mouth found hers instantly, a searing hot kiss that sent electricity sparking through her body. The kiss was hot and demanding this time, and she didn't know whether it was his need or hers that had escalated it.

She shifted against him, trying to stay still, but unable to contain the need he was stoking inside her. His hand continued to stroke her belly, but he didn't move it lower. She wanted him to try again. She wanted him to touch her. Just for a brief moment. Just to know what it felt like again.

Without intending to, without making the decision, she found her fingers wrapping around his wrist again. His hand stilled, just as it had before. His mouth stilled on hers as well.

No, no, no. That wasn't what she'd meant. Nervously, almost afraid of what she wanted, and of whether he might reject her, she moved his hand lower, over her scarred belly, sliding their hands past the waistband of her jeans.

For a moment, he didn't respond. Heat flared in her cheeks. What had she been thinking? Mortified, she tugged on his wrist, but this time, for the first time, he ignored her silent request. Instead, he slipped his fingers beneath the waistband of her boring, cotton underwear and slid through her curls.

She swallowed, suddenly nervous, but before she could think about it, he took her mouth in a devastating kiss of unilateral possession. She wanted to turn around in his arms and kiss him, but his forearm across her breasts kept her still, pinned against him, so all she could do was turn her head. His kiss was hot and demanding, no longer holding back, shattering all her defenses. She kissed him back, desperate for what he could give her, but as soon as she kissed him, he slipped his fingers between her damp folds.

Again, he swallowed her gasp with his kiss, his fingers moving with skilled finesse, stirring up responses she hadn't thought she was capable of anymore. Her body was slick beneath his fingers, responding to him, but he didn't abate with his kisses, and his forearm pressed more tightly against her nipples.

Every part of her body was on fire, an inferno setting her body ablaze. It had been so long, so unbearably long since she'd been with a man, since she'd trusted one enough to allow him to be close to her. She barely knew Jace, but at the same time, she knew so much about him. She understood his intense loyalty, his unflagging moral code, and the guilt that weighed him down every step he took. She knew that somehow he was standing there, holding her, when his injuries should have dragged him down. He was the courage she sought in her own life, the loyalty she tried to have to those who mattered to her, the strength she needed so badly.

He deepened the kiss, turning it from passion into something deeper. Something more. A claiming. As he kissed her, his fingers slipped inside her, making her entire body clench with desire. He was merciless and unrelenting as he touched her, his kisses unending, his fingers moving with constant, delicate perfection. She shifted against him, her hips moving on their own. A small cry slipped from her lips, but he absorbed the sound with his kiss, moving his fingers across her most sensitive bud, harder and faster until—

The orgasm hit her with shocking force. Her body shook, and her legs almost gave out as it rocked through her, seizing her with ruthless, searing fire. Jace held her up, never breaking the kiss, as she twisted against him, fighting to stay upright, trying to find a way to somehow hold in the screams tearing at her throat. He pressed the heel of his hand to her folds, prolonging the climax, and somehow giving her the strength to hold it inside her when all she wanted to do was succumb.

It felt like forever until it finally eased, releasing her into his arms in an exhausted, depleted state. Abby rested her head against him, trying to catch her breath as Jace withdrew his hand from her pants, setting it back upon her stomach. Once again, he spread his fingers across her scars, as if he were trying to pour his own strength into her battered body.

She closed her eyes, heat filling her cheeks as she listened to the sound of wolves searching Kiernan's cabin. Had she really just done that? Let Jace give her an orgasm while standing on a dark stairway. On the other side of the door was a pack hunting them, and somewhere below them were a trio of shifters. It was so not her, but at the same time, there was something incredibly liberating about it.

She'd broken every sensible rule, and she'd allowed

Jace to touch her in a way she hadn't let anyone in a long, long time. She'd trusted him enough to stop paying attention to the wolves, and to turn herself over to him completely. She'd trusted him enough to let him see what she was really like, to give him the chance to reject her...and he hadn't.

Jace pressed a kiss to the side of her neck again, eliciting a small smile from her. This moment was their secret, an intimacy in the silent darkness. Somehow, it felt less real in the dark, in the silence, without a word spoken. Maybe it should have felt more impersonal, but it had been the opposite. Intensely erotic, deeply powerful, a connection that hadn't needed sight or sound to ignite it.

She reached behind her and slid her hand through his silky soft hair. As she did, he turned his head into her arm and kissed the inside of her forearm, a tender, intimate kiss that made her heart turn over. Who kissed the inside of a woman's forearm? It was so personal, so intimate, so...tender.

"I think they're gone." Jace's whisper in her ear made her jump. Belatedly, she realized that the sounds from the cabin had ceased. "Let's head down."

A part of her wanted to refuse to move. She wanted to stay in the darkness with him, in a fantasy world where real life was replaced by intimacy and security, by a sense of connection that wasn't distorted by the wounds of the past, or the uncertainty of the future.

But when he took her hand to guide her down the steps, she didn't resist. As much as she wanted to hide, she couldn't. Real life actually existed, and Seth was out there somewhere, with less than forty hours left of his humanity, unless they found him first.

Chapter Twelve

JACE TIGHTENED HIS fingers around Abby's hand as they reached the bottom of the stairs, drawing her slightly behind him. Drake had reassured him telepathically that they were safe, but he wasn't taking any chances.

He was well aware of the trust that Abby had offered him in the stairwell when she'd allowed him to touch her scars. His heart had ached for her fear, and it had taken all his self-control not to open the sliding door and tear out into the room after Lucius.

If he had, he would have exposed Abby to the vicious bastard who'd attacked her, and there was no fucking chance he was going to do that. So, he'd stayed still, focusing on Abby to distract himself from the fury raging through him that the bastard was roaming free.

He'd kissed Abby's neck to take away her fear, and to distract himself, but the minute he'd tasted her, every cell in his body had responded with need so intense that he'd almost lost control completely. He'd never craved a woman the way he wanted Abby. He wanted her, and his wolf burned for her.

When she'd come apart in his arms, all he'd wanted to do was sink himself inside her and claim her as his, to declare to the world that she was his to protect and cherish.

But he knew that was not a choice he could afford to make. He was still on the edge, a deadly weapon at the mercy of one song, a song she knew intimately. His body was a battlefield, barely able to stay vertical, and he was a murderer who'd stolen her own sister.

He had no business touching her the way he had, but that was too damn bad. She was the light to his darkness, somehow trusting him with her body despite all he was. She fucking *knew* what he'd done, and yet she'd still welcomed his touch, accepting intimacy he was pretty sure she'd hid from since the attack by Lucius.

He didn't know why she'd chosen him. He had no fucking idea why, and as much as he believed he should stay away from her, he couldn't, not as long as she was in danger and her nephew needed his help.

They reached the bottom of the stairs, and she opened the door. As she opened it, light filtered through the opening, blinding him momentarily.

"Kiernan!" Abby slipped past him, racing into the room. Jace propped himself against the door, using the wall to hold himself up as he watched Drake, the female shifter, and a man he didn't know cluster around the injured shifter, who was on a cot much like the one he'd been on upstairs.

Drake. Jace wanted to stop Abby from getting close to the other males, but his body wouldn't respond. His good leg was shaking, and his injured one was useless.

Drake looked up, and immediately stepped in Abby's path, smoothly deflecting her as she reached for the unfamiliar male. "He's healing. Let him be."

Abby immediately stopped, her hand on Drake's arm. Jace fixated on her hand, his wolf suddenly tense as he watched the way her fingers wrapped around Drake.

Drake glanced sharply at Jace, and then his eyes widened. He carefully removed Abby's hand from his arm, and stepped back. *She's all yours, mate. Tell your wolf to stand down.*

Jace swore. He was broadcasting? He should have better discipline than that. He dragged the door closed behind him as he quickly took in the situation. The room was simple and barren, but clean. Doors and a long hallway suggested that it was a sizeable space, extending deep underground.

He reached out with his senses, checking for other inhabitants, but he didn't find any. *We alone?* He knew Drake would have searched out the entire lair the moment he arrived.

Yep. We're good. Drake was still standing between Abby and the others, but he was watching Jace. *You look like hell.*

I'm better than the poor bastard Kiernan's working on. But as he said it, Jace found himself sliding down the doorjamb to the floor. He sat hard, unable to contain his grunt of pain as he landed. Now that the adrenaline was fading, the pain was setting in, and it was coming hard.

He leaned his head back against the door and closed his eyes, trying to focus enough to reach inside him and assess his injuries. As a shifter, he had extensive healing capacities, but he hadn't had time to work on it. He trusted Drake implicitly, and if the other wolf said the place was safe, then it was. There were only two wolves he truly trusted, and Drake was one of them.

He checked his ankle first, grimly assessing the damage. It was as bad as he'd thought. The bones were completely shattered, pulverized into fragments and dust. Not healable. *Fuck.* The enormity of the situation settled on him like a crushing weight. How the hell could he keep Abby safe from Lucius on *one leg*?

He couldn't.

Swearing under his breath, he concentrated on his ankle, pouring healing energy into it, refusing to concede defeat. "Come on," he muttered.

A light hand touched his shoulder, making him start. He grabbed it even as he opened his eyes. Abby was crouched in front of him, her eyes dark with worry. "Jace. I want you to meet Kiernan."

Beside her was the unfamiliar shifter. He was early thirties, strapping and strong. A powerful wolf that exuded dominance. He was wearing jeans and a tattered tee shirt that didn't hide the unrivaled strength of his frame. He had one hand on Abby's shoulder, possessively marking her as his.

Jace sat up quickly, his wolf roaring in fury. "Don't touch her," he snarled.

Kiernan's eyes narrowed, and Abby's mouth dropped open in shock. Shit. What had he just done? He knew what he'd done. He'd claimed her. Marked her as his own in front of a competitor. He had no business doing that, but he couldn't make himself retract it. He just met Kiernan's gaze, letting the other shifter feel the full force of his power and his claim.

For a moment, Kiernan didn't move, then Abby quickly moved to Jace's other side, away from Kiernan, breaking the tension. Kiernan, Jace noticed, didn't try to stop her.

Smart move.

Abby put her hand on Jace's shoulder, squeezing gently. "Kiernan," she said softly. "Jace needs help. His ankle and his arm."

Jace narrowed his eyes at the shifter, unwilling to submit to a wolf he didn't know. "Who are you?"

"I heal." The shifter gave no other answer, but Jace could feel a humming vibration in his ankle, as if he'd already started working on Jace's leg.

"I didn't give you permission," he snapped. He didn't like this at all. He was in this shifter's lair, injured, and the only one who could vouch for him was Abby, who hadn't even been sure he was trustworthy. For all he knew, Kiernan would pull out a recording of that song and—

Shit.

He'd be fucked. He was locked in a basement with a bunch of shifters that he could turn on in a split second. What if Lucius started blasting the song from upstairs? Would they hear it? How long would it take for Jace to attack them all?

I'm on it. Drake's voice was hard and unyielding.

He locked gazes with Drake, who was standing just behind Kiernan, his hands relaxed by his side, the rest of his body primed and ready to step in. *I don't like this, Drake.*

Drake nodded. *You need help, Jace. If he can help you, take it.* He met Jace's eyes, his expression too knowing about the extent of Jace's injuries. *If he pulls out the song, I'll kill him instantly. And you, if I have to.*

He hated being so weak that he had to put himself in a vulnerable position. It went against every fiber of his body to endanger Abby and Drake because he needed help.

"Jace." Abby touched his shoulder, drawing his attention back to her. "Let him help you. He's gifted. He saved my life."

Jace turned his attention back to Kiernan. He studied the shifter, reaching out with his mind to try to pick up on his energy signature, but he got nothing. He couldn't even catch a scent from him. It was as if he was a mirage, not truly present. "I can't sense you."

"As it should be." Kiernan looked at him, resting one muscular forearm over his knee. "I can help you."

"Why would you?" Jace shot back.

"Because it is my calling." Kiernan's voice was calm and steady. "It is my gift and my curse. You found me, so it is my duty to help."

To his surprise, Jace felt the truth resonating in Kiernan's words. The shifter truly did believe it was his duty, and that was something Jace understood, being driven by his own duty to protect other shifters, to create a pack that would keep them safe. "I accept."

Kiernan nodded, and rose to his feet. Without another word, he walked across the room and disappeared through a door that Jace hadn't even noticed. "Chatty guy," Jace observed.

Abby stood up. "He's waiting for you. Come on."

"Back there?" Jace tried to stand, but it took both Abby and Drake's assistance to get him vertical. His body was shaking, and he could barely focus. He knew his body was going into shock, and that was not a good sign. He'd pushed hard after his injuries, yeah, but he'd done that many times in his life and he'd never hit a wall like this before.

He could barely support himself as they helped him to the other room, and the cot they set him on seemed to come up faster than he expected when he tried to sit down on it. Or maybe he'd gone down too fast. Either way, he knew he was in bad shape.

"Get him on his back." Kiernan's voice was distant, fading, and Jace frowned, trying to stay focused as several sets of hands moved him, rolling him over. Pain shot through him, and he sucked in his breath as his ankle hit the side of the cot.

"Why is he in such bad shape?" Drake asked, but Jace could barely focus on his words.

"There's silver in his blood stream," Kiernan said.

Silver? "How?" It was a tremendous effort to form the words.

"Point of entry was the ankle." Kiernan's hands closed around Jace's leg. A scream of agony tore from Jace's throat, and he fought to get his leg free, but he couldn't move.

He opened his eyes, and saw Drake leaning over him, holding him down. "Get the fuck off me."

Drake glanced at him. "Sorry, Jace. It has to be done."

Kiernan did something to his ankle again, and another scream tore from Jace's throat as the pain ricocheted through him. *Jesus.* He gritted his teeth, sweat streaming down his temples. He'd felt pain before, and he was an expert at managing it, but he'd never felt anything like this before.

"It's incredible he's still functioning." Kiernan sounded impressed, almost in awe. "He should have been dead hours ago. I've never seen anyone be able to compartmentalize silver before, and yet he did it, even with his body under such duress from his other injuries." More pain, and another scream.

Jace arched his back, unable to stop the scream as it tore through him. His mind was fragmenting, shattering into dozens of pieces. Memories flashed through his mind. The screams of the woman he'd killed. Melissa. Dying. Crying. The taste of her blood. His need to kill. The burning, insatiable need to kill—

"Jace." Gentle hands framed his face. "It's Abby. Focus on me."

Her voice was like an angel's whisper, easing the agony trying to consume him. He focused on her green eyes, letting himself be swept away by her voice. Her warmth seemed to wrap around him, a soothing, powerful shield that distanced Kiernan and Drake, leaving him with only Abby. He reached for her, and she took his hand, squeezing tightly.

Pain screamed through his body now, as if Kiernan had released the silver and it was burning him up from the inside out, his blood searing its way through his veins. It felt wrong what he was doing. It felt dangerous. It felt like death. He tried to get up, but Drake was still holding him down. "No," Jace gritted out. "It's wrong. Don't trust him. Stop him."

Drake and Abby looked at each other across Jace's body, and he saw their silent exchange. Then the searing pain slammed into his brain, and darkness descended.

Chapter Thirteen

JACE SNAPPED AWAKE, bolting upright in bed. The room was pitch black, but his eyes adjusted swiftly as he rapidly assessed the situation. Abby was asleep on a chair next to the cot, and Drake was standing guard in the hallway just outside the door. He could sense the other two shifters in a room down the hall, but he couldn't find Kiernan. He sensed no other shifters at all.

The hold was secure.

Some of his tension eased, and Jace took a moment to look around. He was in a windowless, cramped room, less than six feet wide, housing only the cot, and Abby's chair. The night was silent, and quiet, no tension lurking, giving him the chance to breathe again. He was in Kiernan's lair, and it was secure at the moment.

With no pressing danger looming, Jace took a moment to study Abby, watching the rise and fall of her chest as she breathed. She was curled up in the chair, looking tiny and vulnerable. Her hair was tumbling down around her shoulders, falling across her face. He studied the wayward locks, his hand clenching against the instinct to brush the hair back from her face. He remembered the reassuring touch of her hands when Kiernan had been healing him, the way her voice had taken the edge off his agony.

Gentle.

Soft.

Kind.

Unable to resist, Jace rolled onto his side to face her. He cautiously reached across the space between them and brushed the stray lock back from her face. Her hair was soft, like silk, softer than he could remember feeling.

Her eyes flickered open. For a moment, she stared at him sleepily, as if she were still hovering between dreamland and reality. He smiled at her, and something turned over in his chest when she smiled back at him. "How are you?" she asked.

At her question, he suddenly realized that the pain that had been haunting him for so long was absent. He'd reached out with his injured arm...and it was much improved. The scars were shiny, but on their way to healing, and he could tell that the internal damage had been repaired. "Damn. I'm impressed." Then he focused on his shattered ankle. No pain. Frowning, he flexed it. To his shock, it moved easily, with only a dull ache of pain. He sat up, frowning as he moved it again, testing it in every direction. He had full mobility. "Impossible." He leapt off the cot and landed on his right leg. He braced for debilitating pain and a collapse to the floor, but his ankle held up. It trembled under the impact, but he was able to keep it straight and solid with a little focus. The faint ache was astoundingly minimal, easy to compartmentalize. Son of a bitch. *His ankle had been reconstructed. He was back.*

He sank back onto the cot and bowed his head, unable to contain his sudden rush of emotion. *His ankle was healed.* He was strong enough to be the alpha who protected his pack and his mate. He could do what he'd thought he'd never be able to do again.

"Jace?" Abby's hands slid over his bare shoulders. "It didn't work?"

He caught her hand and looked up. She was sitting beside him, her face inches from his. "You did this," he said, his voice hoarse.

Wariness flickered in her eyes. "Did what?"

He slid his hands through her hair, emotions thick in his chest. "My ankle was done. I couldn't be an alpha, or even survive in a pack with a crippled leg. It was over...and now it's fine."

Her face lit up. "It's healed? Really?"

He turned toward her, swinging his legs around her so he flanked her hips. "You did it. You brought me here. You ignored my orders and dragged me to Kiernan." He tunneled his hands through her hair. "You gave me back my life, when all you should have done was hate me." He didn't understand her. He could barely grasp what she'd done for him. He'd resigned himself to his useless leg, and to have it given back to him was overwhelming, a gift he would spend a lifetime trying to be worthy of.

She encircled his wrists with her fingers. "Jace, you need to stop," she said gently. "Hating yourself for what you did allows Grigori to win. You were coerced to do something completely against your nature. If I can see that, why can't you?"

"Because I relive her murder every second of every

day." He tangled his fingers in her hair, needing to ground himself in her. Even as he tried to convince her of his guilt, at the same time, he needed her to argue with him, to not let him win. "I *wanted* to kill her. My wolf thrived on the attack. I felt it inside me, a sense of victory when she died. Do you understand? I became a monster that day. It wasn't simply that I killed her. It was that I *wanted* to do it." The words were ugly, a hateful ugly truth, but he had to say them. He was ashamed of what he'd been, of that truth, but he didn't want to hide from it anymore. Abby had given him so much. She deserved to know who he really was, and what he'd become inside.

Abby sighed, and turned toward him. She slid onto his lap and wrapped her legs around his hips.

Jace stiffened, his body going hard at the intimacy of the position. He pulled his hands from her and held them up, forcing himself not to touch her. "What are you doing?"

She clasped her fingers behind his neck and tried to tug him toward her.

He resisted, his hands still in the air. "Abby. You need to get off my lap. Seriously. Right now." Desire raced through him, a deep, relentless need to slide his hands through her hair and drag her toward him. To sink his mouth onto hers and claim her. To toss her onto his cot and strip off her clothes, layer by layer, until she was all his.

She ignored him. Instead, she leaned into him and pressed her mouth to his. Her lips were soft and tentative, igniting a fierceness inside him he'd never experienced. With a low growl, he opened his mouth, taking her offering with a searing kiss of unrestrained hunger. She wrapped her arms around his neck, kissing him back just as fiercely as he was kissing her. The need was uncontrollable, raging through him with relentless heat. He'd burned for her since the first moment he'd seen her, fighting the battle every moment, but she shattered the last vestiges of his control.

"Kiss me, Jace," she whispered. "I want you."

Another surge of hunger, and his kisses became a frenzied, desperate claiming, far beyond his ability to control them. He needed to touch her, to kiss her, to feel her bare skin beneath his palms. His wolf craved her, and so did the man, unified in their need for the woman in his arms.

Abby was so brave, and yet, at the same time, so vulnerable. Her courage to bring him to Kiernan when Lucius was hunting them astounded him. Her ability to forgive him for the unthinkable was beyond comprehension, a gift he was clinging to desperately. She was brave, but at the same time, she was soft, offering Jace comfort and faith when he deserved none. He was so lost right now, drowning in the chaos his life had become, but she had stood by him, giving him purpose, never judging, never doubting. She saw in him the man he'd thought he was, giving him hope even when he knew he didn't deserve it.

She'd given him so much, and he felt as though he'd only taken in return. He knew he didn't deserve this moment with her. She should be punishing him, not giving him the most precious gift on earth, her faith, her trust, and her kiss. He knew this, but he couldn't make himself break away. He needed what she gave him. He knew that without Abby, he wouldn't still be alive. His soul wouldn't still be hanging together by a sliver, refusing to shatter completely.

He needed Abby in a way he'd never needed anyone or anything. He ran his hands down her spine, beneath her shirt, tracing each bone. Her body was a miracle to him, curvy, soft, and yet strong at the same time. Unrivaled elegance and beauty...and the body of a survivor.

He palmed her belly, pressing his hand against the hard ridges left behind by Lucius. Abby tensed and she stopped kissing him, though she didn't pull back. Suspended in fear, waiting for his next move.

Anger rushed through him, a fierce outrage that Lucius had taken away Abby's understanding of her beauty, stripping away self-confidence in who she was. She was wrong to fear his reaction to her scars. Resolution flooded him, and he shifted, rolling her onto her back on his cot.

The moment her shoulders hit, Jace stretched on top of her, sliding low enough to press a kiss to her stomach. Abby tensed, touching the top of his head. "Jace, you don't have do that—"

He caught her hand and kissed her fingertips. "Look at me, Abby."

She propped herself up on her elbows and looked down at him. The vulnerability on her face made his heart turn over. He pressed another kiss to her stomach, keeping his gaze pinned on her face. "When I look at you, do you know what I see?"

She shook her head once, her gaze riveted to his.

"I look into your eyes, and I see a woman who loved her sister, a woman who's so loyal to those she loves that she's willing to do whatever it takes to keep them safe, including teaming up with the bastard who killed her sister."

Her face softened. "Jace—"

He pressed another kiss to her stomach. "When I

hear your voice, it's as if the angels have gifted me with a moment of perfection, a whisper of peace in a life that doesn't deserve it."

Her eyes began to glisten with unshed tears. "My voice has done so many terrible things," she whispered. "You might feel guilty for killing my sister, but I've been responsible for destroying good men and making them kill hundreds of innocents."

At her words, he finally began to understand why she could look at him and not see a murderer, because she believed she was the one truly at fault. He laughed softly, a laugh filled with the shared pain of causing harm they'd never intended. He moved up her body and kissed her, trying to pour into the kiss the words he couldn't articulate, a kiss that told her that he understood her pain, and that it would never mar the way he saw her.

He broke the kiss, searching her gaze as he pressed his hand to her stomach. "And when I kiss these scars, I see a woman who endured a hell that would have killed most people. I see courage." He kissed her. "And beauty." He kissed her again. "I see a survivor so brave that I'm humbled by the fact you look at me and see anything worthwhile."

A tear trickled down her cheek. "I'm sorry," she whispered. "I'm so sorry that my voice made you do something so terrible. It's not your fault. You need to understand that. It's my fault. I'm the one responsible for my sister's death. I killed her, Jace. *Me.*"

He took away her words with a kiss, using the intimacy to shield them both from the pasts that tormented them so deeply. He palmed her belly again, kneading the ridged flesh with his knuckles, as if he could break apart the scar tissue and give her a second chance at life. He deepened the kiss, pouring himself into it, wanting nothing more than to take away her pain. "Kiss me back, sweetheart. Let yourself feel how incredible I think you are."

Chapter Fourteen

JACE KNEW THE moment Abby succumbed to the kiss. Her body softened, and her arms went around him again, holding him tight against her. With a low growl, Jace moved his hand along her ribs. He slipped his hand under her bra and cupped her breast, flicking his thumb over her nipple.

She twisted under him, a tiny gasp of pleasure escaping from her. He grinned and grasped her shirt, pulling it over her head in one deft move. The moment her shirt was off, his world seemed to stop. He was stunned by the magnificence of her body. Her breasts swelled above the cotton of her sports bra, and he loved the curve of her hip. Her belly bore the marks of her bravery, the beauty of her soul that had survived the abuse, and triumphed over the assault.

Abby put her hand on his arm. "The way you look at me is amazing," she whispered, her eyes shimmering with unshed tears. "I never thought anyone would look at me that way."

Jace stretched out beside her and kissed her, framing her jaw with his hand for a moment, before sliding his palm lower, along her neck. He traced the curve of her collarbone, then let his fingers drift over the cotton of her bra. He hooked his fingers beneath the elastic band, then slipped it up her arms and over her head.

The moment it was off, he palmed her breast, letting the soft flesh fill his hand as he kissed her again. Her skin was soft, almost like silk, her body blessed with all the curves of being a woman. Desire mounted inside him, and his wolf paced restlessly, needing to claim her. Jace held both in check, however, determined to make Abby understand how much he cherished every kiss, every touch, every moment with her.

Still rubbing his fingers across her nipple, Jace kissed her jaw, grazed her earlobe with his teeth, and then scraped them across her collarbone. Abby slid her fingers into his hair, her gentle touch like fire.

Jace kissed his way across her skin, honoring every dip and curve of her body, until he reached her breasts. He swept his tongue across her nipple and then blew gently. Satisfaction surged through him when she shifted restlessly. He could feel she was completely attuned to him, sensitive to his slightest touch, as he was to her.

He slid his hand over her hip and to the waistband of her jeans as he continued to weave magic with his lips on her breasts. When his fingers landed on her zipper, he felt the subtle shift of Abby's hips toward him, accepting his touch, asking for more. He was so connected to her, he could sense every move. It was as if he could feel her soul inside his body, as if every one of her emotions had become a part of him.

He'd never been so connected with another human being. It was surreal, and probably should feel threatening, but it didn't. It made him burn with life and desire, awakening parts of him that had been long dead, or maybe never even alive.

He caught her mouth in another kiss, this one more desperate than the last, as his need for her began to escape the edges of his control. He unfastened her jeans with one hand, and then palmed her stomach, lower this time, his fingers touching the edges of her underwear. Raw, carnal need ate away at him as he recalled touching her on the stairs. She'd been so responsive, completely entrusting herself into his safekeeping. Her orgasm had been a gift, proof that she'd relinquished fear about Lucius so she could focus on Jace, trusting him to alert her if danger mounted.

That was what he lived for: safeguarding those he'd vowed to protect. To have Abby surrender to him so completely when hell was breaking loose around them had awakened in him a fierce, almost savage need to protect her, to rise above the shit that Grigori had thrust him into.

He slipped his hand lower, his fingers tangling in the silken curls and then the damp folds of her body. She gasped his name, but he deepened the kiss, not allowing her space to break free of him. Her hips moved restlessly under his hand, matching the rhythm, inviting the intimacy.

"I need more," he whispered into the kiss. "I need all of you."

She nodded, her fingers going to the waistband of his jeans. Primal need poured through him and he rolled off her, shucking his jeans and tossing them aside. Abby propped herself up on her elbows, her eyes burning with emotion as he grasped her jeans and tugged them down over her hips, taking her underwear along.

He couldn't take his gaze off hers as he slid her pants over her feet. They dropped to the floor with a soft thud, and then he lowered himself on top of her, letting their skin touch inch by tantalizing inch. Her breasts brushed his bare chest. His thighs settled on hers. His cock rested on her stomach. The sensation of her body against his was electric, a whirring hum of sparks shooting through him, eliciting searing awareness in every nerve.

Abby smiled and slid her arms around his neck. "Amazing," she whispered.

"Perfection," he agreed, as he bent down to kiss her.

Her lips were soft, but her kiss was bold and courageous, stripping him of what little resistance he still had left. He was insatiably aroused by her vulnerability and courage, but her boldness undid him. With a low growl that was more wolf than man, he slid his knee between hers to part her legs. She locked her ankles around his hips, a statement of such trust that his throat actually tightened. With Abby, it didn't feel like sex. The physical attraction was undeniable, but it was so much more with her. He felt like the physical need thundering through him was driven by his soul's need to connect with hers, not just the way her body felt against his.

His cock ached with need, and his muscles were trembling with the effort of holding back, but he would not take her before she was ready. He wanted to make this more than right for her. He wanted to make it a moment that would heal all the broken fragments of her soul and wipe away all the remnants that Lucius had left behind.

He kissed her again, more deeply, summoning all the tenderness he'd had to shed when he became alpha. He reached inside, trying to find the softness that he wasn't allowed to have, while he slid his hand over her hip, tracing designs on her skin. Her fingers tightened in his hair, and he felt her body soften under his as she allowed herself to merge with him, allowing them to merge into a perfect union.

She was damp and ready for him, and he knew he couldn't wait anymore. He tightened his grip on her hair and then adjusted his hips so his cock was pressed against her entrance. He wanted to keep kissing her, but even more, he wanted to see her face, and he wanted her to see his. He needed her to ground herself in him, to know that the man she was with treasured her. He broke the kiss and pulled back, just enough to be able to make eye contact. "You need to know something," he said, as he moved his hips, pressing more tightly against her.

Her eyebrows went up. "And what's that?"

"I will always protect you. You're mine now, and that means you will never have to fight your battles alone." As he spoke, he sank inside her, connecting them the only way that mattered.

She gripped his shoulders, shifting as he drove deeper. "You don't need to say that, Jace. I want this as much as you do. It doesn't have to come with promises—"

Anger rushed through him, a deep fury that she actually believed that. "Wrong." He stilled his hips, forcing himself to stop, refusing to continue until she understood the truth. "This *does* have to come with promises. You matter. You deserve to be worshipped, not used and tossed aside." His fingers tightened in her hair, and urgency coursed through him. "Don't *ever* say that this doesn't have to come with promises. There's no other way. You need to understand that. You deserve promises, and you have them from me."

Her brow furrowed as she listened. "You mean that," she whispered, her voice soft with wonder.

"Damn right." He drove deep again, satisfaction rolling through him when she gasped. "I've been living as an alpha for years. My job has been to protect and lead, not to feel or care, but you've reached inside me and ripped apart the shields keeping me focused. You make me want to be a better man, not just a better alpha." He framed her face. "When you look at me, you see the man I want to be, the one I've been trying to be for so long. You make me feel like I have a chance. You matter, and *this* matters." He buried himself even more deeply inside her, and she gasped again, her fingers digging into his shoulders.

He grabbed her hand and set it on his chest, over his heart. "Tell me you feel this." His heart was thundering, and it felt hot, as if the wolf inside him was clawing to get out.

Her eyes widened, and she nodded. "I do." She spread her palm across his chest. "It feels like I'm touching your soul."

"You are."

Her face softened. "Thank you, Jace."

He framed her cheeks with his hands and kissed her, summoning the most tender, most passionate, most honest kiss he could summon, trying to let her see everything he was and everything he wanted to be. She wrapped her arms around him and held him to her, accepting his kiss, and offering him the same.

His throat tightened, and for a split second, he

couldn't breathe. He felt as though he needed to wrap himself around her, threading his soul through hers until they were so tangled that they'd never come undone.

She gasped and arched beneath him, her hips moving in a tantalizing rhythm with his. He braced his palms by her shoulders, his muscles flexing as he thrust again and again, the heated coils within him twisting tighter and tighter until—

"Jace!" Abby gasped his name, her body tensing as the orgasm ripped through her, dragging Jace ruthlessly with her. He bucked against her, holding onto her as the orgasm claimed him, ricocheting back and forth between them until all that existed was an unending cycle of climax and completion, again and again until finally, mercifully, it released them both.

Jace sank down beside her, keeping most of his body on top of hers, just allowing his weight to settle on the cot. She snuggled against him, tucking herself into the shield of his body as they both fought to catch their breath. Perspiration was glistening on her body, giving it a magical sheen that almost did justice to the enormity of what had just happened.

What *had* just happened? He felt as though he'd fallen thousands of feet through a vortex, being spun ruthlessly around and around, until he had no equilibrium, no foundation, and no sense of where he was supposed to be. Except he knew exactly where he was supposed to be: right there, with Abby, and nowhere else.

Chapter Fifteen

ABBY RESTED HER head on Jace's shoulder, tucking herself up against him. His arm was around her, his fingers gently playing with her hair. She sighed, amazed at how relaxed and at peace she was. Her body had been strung with tension for so long she'd forgotten what it felt like to be able to breathe deeply and let herself relax into the mattress.

It was because of Jace, and everything he offered her. She ran her hand over his chiseled chest, still in awe of his physical perfection. He was elemental beauty and grace, everything Abby wasn't, and yet, he'd made her feel like she was the oxygen he needed in order to breathe.

She spread her palm out on his chest, counting the beats of his heart. His skin was still hot, the warmth pouring into her like the warm sunlight on a cold day. Was that his wolf energy? Or just his own inner strength as a man?

He put his hand over hers, trapping it. She watched his fingers encircle hers, his strong hand dwarfing hers.

"You make me feel safe," she said quietly. "After Lucius, I was afraid all the time. I felt as though he was in the shadows, stalking me, ready to attack at any moment."

His fingers tightened around hers, and he brought her hand to his mouth, pressing a kiss to each knuckle. "I want you to feel safe," he said, his voice equally as soft. "I'll do whatever it takes to protect you, but we can't ignore the truth."

She frowned. "What truth?"

He rolled onto his side to face her, draping his leg over her hip. "The fact that if I hear that song, I *will* shift and kill." He traced his finger along her jaw. "You're safe with me now. I promise you that. But that song..." He shook his head. "It owns me."

Guilt settled deep in her chest. She knew he spoke the truth, because she'd seen so many wolves try to fight it, and all had failed. But she'd also seen something else. She'd seen Grigori, Lucius, and Damien learn to defeat it, because their drive for control and dominance was so strong. Jace had the same inner drive, but his was protection and safety of others...of her. Could a good heart be strong enough to defeat it, the way a black heart was? "It's not that simple," she said.

"Because Grigori and Damien have managed it." His words were grim, his jaw tight as he acknowledged that they had succeeded where he hadn't. "Tell me about Grigori. I need to know it all. Why is he after you? Why Lucius?"

She sighed, not wanting to go there, but knowing she needed to. She couldn't hide from the nightmares anymore. Grigori had Seth, and the only way to get him back was to face it. She focused on the warmth of

Jace's leg over her hip, and in the intimacy between them that somehow kept the darkness of her past at bay. "My mom was Grigori's mate when he was young. They met when she was fifteen, and he was twenty-five. He was the son of the pack alpha, powerful, handsome, and charming. He was captivated by her beauty, and he claimed her. She was swept up by him and fell for him immediately. She was sixteen when she had my sister."

Jace's eyebrows went up, and he ran his hand down her arm and over her hip, as if he sensed that she needed him to ground her. "And you?"

She nodded. "She was eighteen when she had me. She'd been so young and innocent when she first met Grigori, that she couldn't see how depraved Grigori and his father were. She was completely under his spell." She bit her lip, focusing on Jace's eyes to ground herself. "I saw so many terrible things," she said. "They loved to torture innocents. Men, women, children. It didn't matter. It was—" She shook her head to clear it. "When I was seven, my nightmares were constant. I was terrified that Grigori would come into my room at night and take me, like he'd done to the others. I started singing to distract myself, then one day..." She stopped, as images of that terrible night flashed through her mind.

"Look at me, Abby." Jace's voice was gentle, drawing her gaze to him. His eyes were blazing with barely contained anger, but she knew it was toward Grigori. Somehow, his anger chased away the fear, cocooning her in his strength.

She held up her hand, and he took it, sliding his fingers between hers before bringing her hand to his lips and lightly kissing it. "Continue," he said softly, between kisses.

She watched his lips press against her skin, focusing on him instead of the memories. "I was hiding in the trees near a clearing where they'd staked out a male shifter and his two daughters. I was so scared for them, and for myself, so I started to sing. I knew they wouldn't hurt me, because I was Grigori's daughter, and therefore he was the only one allowed to hurt me. I thought singing would help bring them peace, but instead—" She stopped.

Jace slipped his hand behind her neck and kissed her, his mouth tender and demanding at the same time. He didn't stop the kiss, continuing until she melted against him, her body crying out for his touch. He broke the kiss and began to nibble down the side of her neck. "Let me guess. Your song made the dad shift and attack the others. Grigori or his dad saw it happen, figured out your talent, and decided to use you."

She closed her eyes, focusing on the way his teeth grazed her earlobe. "They told me if I didn't do it, that they'd hurt my mom or my sister." She pulled back. "I should have been brave. I should have told my mom and trusted that she'd run away with me, but she was so caught up in Grigori's spell that I didn't know if she would support me. So, I said nothing. There were so many, Jace, so many. I just—"

God, how many times had she stood there, that terrible song coming from her mouth, while men shifted and destroyed innocents. The screams of pain from the victims, the agony of the men after it was over and they'd shifted back, realizing what they'd done. "He wanted to break them," she whispered. "Sometimes it turned them into lethal disciples, and other times..." She looked at Jace. "It destroyed their soul. Like you. I saw it in your eyes at the trial. You were like the others. You felt that same anguish that they had, and yet somehow, you were still functioning, still caring, still fighting to find meaning in it. You may think you're weak, Jace, but you're the opposite. No one else who felt your anguish was able to survive the weight on their soul." She rested her palm on his heart. "Just you," she whispered. "You're special." Her throat tightened as she said the words, and she knew it was true. "You're the first one, the only one, who survived my song without losing who you were."

His eyes darkened, and yearning flashed through them, a deep, raw craving for her to be right. She knew how deeply he needed to be whole again, to find a way to believe in himself. She realized she was his only chance for that, the only one who truly understood what he'd endured and how strong he was to be lying there with her, fighting for survival, even though he was willing to die.

He didn't acknowledge his own needs, however. He simply brushed her hair back from her face, offering her comfort, as if he truly understood what she'd gone through, the depth of anguish she lived with every day for what she'd allowed Grigori to force her to do. "What finally made you leave the pack?" he asked gently.

"When Lucius decided to marry my sister. I knew what he was like, but my sister fell for his charms the same way my mom had fallen for Grigori. She hadn't seen what I'd seen. She'd never been there when Lucius and Grigori had forced me to sing to those innocent men..." She blinked back tears. "When I found out that my sister was going to marry Lucius, I tried to tell her the truth. She didn't want to believe me, so she confronted Lucius."

Jace groaned. "Oh...hell..."

She nodded. "That's when he attacked me. It was my punishment for interfering. My grandmother found me, and she took me to Kiernan." Tears burned in her eyes. "My grandmother told my mother what had happened, and my mom believed her." She looked at him. "*She believed her*. All this time, I'd kept the truth from them, thinking I was protecting them, thinking that they would never believe me, and I'd been wrong. I should have had faith in them, Jace, but I didn't. My mom told my sister what Lucius had done, and this time, my sister finally accepted the truth. Together, they tried to break from the pack, but Grigori found my mom. He killed her, torturing her to tell him where my sister and I were, but she never told."

She looked at him. "I spent all that time letting Grigori control me because I didn't believe in my mom. If I'd told her, she would have left right away, and they'd both still be alive. I was afraid, and after Lucius, I was still afraid. She died for me, and yet, all along, I didn't think she'd even believe me. I was so wrong...and my lack of belief in her, in both of them, resulted in them both dying."

"It's not your fault." He took her hand and pressed a kiss to her palm, his eyes flashing. "You're like me, a natural protector. Your number one goal was to ensure the safety of those you loved. You'd been raised in the pack since birth, trained to believe in their omnipotence. The fact that you were able to see what they'd done and stand up to them in the end is a testament to your incredible strength."

"Me?" She laughed softly, a laugh of bitterness. "I was stupid—"

"No." He caught her jaw, forcing her to look at him. His face was angry, and his eyes were glittering. "You're fucking amazing. Never, ever blame yourself for singing that song. Ever. They were holding the ones you loved most hostage, and you were a girl, in the hands of brutal killers. You survived it, and you never lost your ability to love. Your sister and your mother were perfectly capable of seeing what was going on. They chose not to, until you were almost killed. But you didn't hide from what was happening. You saw it all along. Do you understand how much courage it took to see the truth, when everyone around you didn't want to?"

Tears filled her eyes as she searched his face, her heart turning over at his words. "You make me sound... brave," she whispered. She couldn't stop a tear from trickling down her cheek. The only emotions she'd ever felt for herself were hate, disgust, horror, and guilt. But with the way Jace was looking at her, suddenly, she felt different, like maybe, just maybe, there was something inside her that was as beautiful as what she saw in him. "And then came you..."

She laid her hand on his bare chest. "You see me in a way that I've always wished I was, but never thought I could be. You make me...feel like I can breathe, like I deserve to breathe. In your arms, I feel safe, and I've never felt safe in my entire life. You are this great treasure, this great source of strength and yet..." Her fingers dug into his chest. "At any moment, I could trigger you and force you to kill me. The ugliness is so close to the surface."

"For both of us." He slid his hands through her hair. "I am your greatest threat, and you are mine, and yet...I feel like you're my only chance to survive."

She searched his face. "That's how I feel too."

He framed her face with his hands. "Listen to me, Abby. No matter what happens going forward, you can't blame yourself. Not for the choices you already made, or what might happen in the future. You have an amazing heart, and a beautiful soul, both of which somehow survived a childhood of corruption and depravity. Don't ever lose that, okay? No matter what." He put his hand over her heart. "If you hold onto that, then Lucius and Grigori lose, regardless of whatever else happens." Heat poured from his hand to her heart, melting the shields that had been around it for so long. "I would be dead right now, by my own hand, if you hadn't walked up to me and asked for my help, refusing to let me die. I need you, and I owe you. I want to destroy the demons that haunt you, and I want to help you retrieve Seth." His eyes darkened. "I want to be that man for you, Abby. I need to do that."

Her throat tightened, and she nodded. "Okay," she whispered. She didn't even know how to ask for help, or to accept it, but somehow, Jace made it easier. Maybe it was because she understood the demons that haunted him, and she knew that he needed her as much as she needed him. "What do we do now? Seth is out there somewhere, and in two days, Grigori and Lucius are going to force him to kill using my voice. I can't let that happen." She rolled onto her back and pressed her palms to her eyes, trying to regroup. As much as she wanted this moment to just be about her and Jace finding a place to leave their guilt and torment behind, it was more than that. "We have to stop it, Jace."

"I understand. I'm with you." His voice was taut, almost feral in his fury. "Tell me why your song didn't turn Damien in the alley."

She rolled onto her side to face him. "Because they practiced, again and again, and again."

A muscle ticked in his cheek. "They listened to your song repeatedly until they finally learned to resist it?"

She nodded.

"How many people did they kill before they beat it?"

"Hundreds, at least, but—" She caught Jace's arm as he swore. "But I truly believe that's because they didn't really care if they killed. They were learning to resist for strategic purposes, but they *liked* killing, and a part of them didn't want to stop. You're different."

"I'm not that different—"

"Jace!" She smacked him in the chest. "Don't say that! Don't you understand what they're like? Didn't you see my scars? Lucius did that for *pleasure*. How can you say you're like that? Don't insult me like that!"

He swore and caught her arm. "Hey, I'm sorry." He wiped his thumb over her cheek, and belatedly she realized she was crying. "You're right. I'm not like them."

She wrapped her fingers around his wrist, unable to stop the tears. "Don't take my faith away from me," she whispered. "I haven't trusted a man my whole life, until you. Don't tell me I'm wrong. I need my faith in you. I need to know that there's someone good out there in this world. Do you understand?"

He nodded, continuing to stroke her cheek. "I understand." He leaned forward and kissed her gently, a kiss so tender and kind that more tears threatened.

She closed her eyes, letting his lips drift over her cheeks, kissing away the tears. He cupped her face gently, so gently, his thumb tracing delicate circles along her jaw while he nibbled at her lips. Her soul ached for his touch, for his kiss, for the safety of his embrace, for how he made her feel.

She ached for *him*.

Chapter Sixteen

JACE CONTINUED TO kiss her as he slid his hand over her hip, tracing the curve of her body with such a delicate touch it was as if his fingers were no more than a feather whispering over her skin. The turmoil inside her began to subside, calmed by his kiss and his touch, by the feel of his strong body stretched out beside her.

She spread her fingers over his chest again, losing herself in the heat of his presence and the magic of his kiss.

"Yes," he whispered, "touch me. It's okay. Anything you want to do is okay."

After a lifetime of being commanded and threatened, his words seemed to pour lightness into her heart. She slipped her hand behind his head, pulling him closer. He moved over her, deepening the kiss as he settled on top of her, his ripped body pinning her to the cot. She was trapped beneath him, but she didn't feel afraid. Jace made her feel safe, even though she knew he could kill her in a heartbeat if he heard the song. But somehow, someway, she believed he would never hurt her. There was just something about him, an inner strength, a mortal fierceness, and the ache of regret that made him stronger than anything Grigori and Lucius could throw back at him.

She wrapped her legs around his hips, drawing him closer as he continued to kiss her, his lips and tongue a beautiful array of sensuality, lust, and intimacy. She felt as though each kiss was chasing away another shadow, another memory, another horror from her past. Telling him had brought them to the surface, and his kisses were severing their grip on her, allowing her to breathe again.

He cupped her face, drawing back enough to see her as he shifted his hips, sinking more intimately between her legs. "You make me feel like the man I want to be," he said.

Her heart tightened. "All my life, I've been responsible for terrible things happening to good people. To know that I bring good into your life, even if it's just a little bit, is amazing. I didn't know I could do that."

"You do." He tunneled his fingers through her hair, bracing himself with his elbows on either side of her head. "I was ready to die that day at your grandmother's house, and you gave me a reason to live." He grinned as he shifted, thrusting inside her.

She gasped, unable to keep herself from shifting in response. It felt so incredible to be connected to him so intimately, to have him gazing at her as if he wanted them both to know exactly who they were with. Her heart ached, an ache that hurt as much as it healed. "I love you, Jace," she whispered, the words so quiet she barely even heard them. She didn't mean to say them, but they slipped out, pouring out into the space between them.

Jace stilled, his face going blank for a split second.

She caught her breath, suddenly afraid. Afraid she would drive him away. Afraid that by saying the words, by admitting to herself that she'd let herself care, that she was going to find her heart carved apart once again. It wasn't safe to love. She knew that. She didn't want to be there again, loving someone so much that she made terrible choices to protect them. "I didn't say that," she said, trying desperately to recant. "Please, I can't afford that—"

"You gave it to me. It's mine, now. I can't pretend you didn't say it." He kissed her again, deep, fierce, and claiming. As he kissed her, he began to thrust again, slowly at first, then faster, deeper, until the rhythm of their bodies became a thundering percussion of music that filled even the darkest, most hidden, most protected recesses of her soul. He was merciless and rough, but at the same time, there was such tenderness in his kiss and his lovemaking that her heart swelled in response, crying out for him, for how he made her feel, for how much he mattered to her.

The orgasm swept over her with merciless power, driving deep into her heart and shredding the last remains of denial she was clinging to. She arched back, clinging to Jace's shoulders as he bucked against her, succumbing to the same orgasm that had consumed her. His fingers sliding through her hair as he found her mouth, claiming her on all levels as the last shocks of their climax shuddered through her.

Tears burned her eyes as he collapsed on top of her, pressing his face into the crook of her neck. Abby wrapped her arms around him, holding him to her, unable to stop the tears streaming down her cheeks as the truth settled on her. It was too late. There was no going back. She'd fallen deeply, completely in love with this maddening, honorable, broken man who could doom her. If she sang to him, if she broke *his* soul by making him kill again, she wouldn't survive it...which meant that she would do whatever it took to protect him from her...no matter what the cost.

* * *

He liked listening to her breathe.

Jace lay beside Abby, his hand on her belly, unwilling to shift positions and take the chance of awakening her. After they'd made love the second time, she'd fallen asleep in his arms, tucked up against him as if he were her shield to the world.

She was breathing in a slow, steady rhythm, the kind of deep breathing that told him that she was completely relaxed, trusting him to keep her safe. Wonder rolled over him as he brushed a kiss over her hair, still amazed by how soft and delicate the curls were. She was half his size, so small he could crush her easily, awakening in him a fierce protectiveness.

He'd always been protective of anyone he sensed needed help, but Abby was different. She called to him on a deeper level, as if she could touch the hidden part of him that drove every action he'd ever taken.

The scars on her belly were smooth and hard as he traced them. He'd thought she was a survivor when he'd first felt those scars, but now that he knew all that she'd endured before that point, he knew differently. She was the strongest human being he'd ever met, and her beautiful heart had been ruthlessly crushed until it shouldn't even beat anymore...except it did.

And it beat for him.

His fingers tightened on her belly as he recalled the moment she'd whispered those surreal words. *I love you, Jace.* She loved him. After all he'd done, after all he was destined to do, she'd gifted him with her *love.*

Jace rolled onto his back and clasped his hands behind his head, staring blankly at the ceiling while he went over that moment again. In her sleep, Abby scooted closer, tucking herself against him again, not allowing him distance.

Instinctively, he lowered one arm to wrap it around her shoulder, pulling her even more tightly against him. Since he'd killed Melissa, he'd been able to see no truth other than that he was a murderer, and a walking time bomb. He'd known it was his duty to end his life before he could be turned again...but it was different now.

Abby believed in him. She needed him, both to help her, and also to restore her faith in humanity, and men. If he died, if he let that fucking song take him, he would betray her on both levels. If he died or killed because of her song, it would stain her soul, not just his. He could not let the song win, or it would break her.

"I can't do that to you," he whispered, brushing his lips across her heart. "You leave me no choice."

She stirred in his arms and blinked at him sleepily. "What are you talking about?"

He took a deep breath. "Do you remember when you said that maybe I could build immunity to the song?"

She nodded slowly, the sleepy fog fading from her eyes.

He couldn't believe he was saying this, but he could see no other way. "Will you help me try?"

Her eyes widened, and she sat up. The sheet fell away from her breasts, but she didn't seem to notice. "You want me to sing to you?"

"Not here. Not where you aren't safe from me, but...yeah." He met her gaze. "If we're going to go after Seth, and if I'm going to keep you safe from Lucius and Grigori, I have to be able to handle the song. I swear I'll make sure I can't hurt you when you sing, but——"

Her eyes lit up. "Yes." She nodded reverently. "Of course I'll help."

Hope leapt through him. "Aren't you afraid?"

She set her hand on his jaw, sliding her fingers along his whiskers. "Of course I'm scared," she said solemnly. "I'm actually terrified, of many things, including wolf shifters...except you. I'm not scared of you, and I never will be, no matter what."

This time, instead of cringing away from her vote of confidence, resolution flooded him, a fierce determination to do whatever it took to prevail. "Then let's do it."

Before she could answer, a heavy knock sounded on the door. "Jace." Drake's voice was low and rough. "You better get out here. Now."

* * *

Still buttoning her jeans, Abby hurried after Jace as he strode out of his room. Drake was leaning against the wall of the hallway waiting for them, his arms folded over his chest. His muscles were bunched, his expression tense, making him look every bit the deadly shifter bodyguard. His dark eyes flicked knowingly from Jace to her, and Abby's cheeks heated up.

Of course Drake would know what they'd been doing. Everyone there would have known. They were all shifters, which meant they had heightened senses. She hadn't even been thinking of that at the time, but now she realized that everyone had known exactly what they were doing, the entire time they were doing it.

Jace reached behind him and took her hand. He squeezed gently and pulled her up beside him so he could put his arm around her shoulders, clearly marking her as his as he turned toward Drake. "What's going on?"

Drake glanced at Abby again, but this time, he nodded in acknowledgement, accepting her position with Jace. "This way." He turned and strode down the hallway toward the living room.

Abby started to follow him, but Jace stopped and turned her toward him. He caught her chin, forcing her to look up at him. "Never hide from what we have," he said, his voice low. "We stand together, no matter what. Understand?"

Relief rushed through her, and she smiled. "You're sort of bossy," she teased.

He stared at her for a moment, as if processing her response, then a slow grin spread across his face. "Yeah, well, I'm alpha. These things happen."

"Well, here's the thing." She started walking, and tossed him a haughty look over her shoulder. "I spent my life being bossed around by wolves, so I don't want another alpha. Equality sounds good to me."

His grin widened, and he snagged her wrist, dragging her back toward him. She bumped into his chest, but before she could protest, he sank his mouth onto hers and kissed her. It was a deep, penetrating kiss designed to make her collapse under the assault.

It worked.

By the time he drew back, her legs were trembling and her heart was pounding. He grinned smugly. "Alpha," he said. "I like it that way."

She wasn't going to lie. She rather liked him the way he was, too. But at the same time, the reason she liked him that way was because she knew that his alpha posturing was a lie when it came to her. He'd never force her to do anything, which was why she felt safe with him. So, she simply slipped her hand in his and smiled at him. "Liar," she said softly. "You like that I give you grief. I know you do."

He blinked with feigned innocence. "What?"

"You're not alpha with me, but it's okay. I won't tell anyone." She wiggled her eyebrows at him as she began to walk down the hall, towing him behind her.

After a moment, he sighed in capitulation and lengthened his stride to catch up to her. He caught her around the waist and trapped her against the wall, his eyes feral with hunger. "You make me more dangerous than I've ever been," he growled. "I want to claim you, and defend you, and not be nice about it." He slid his fingers along her jaw. "And at the same time, I want to be tender for you. Soft. Gentle. I want to be the silk that slides over your body, and the dragon who claims you for all eternity. I want it all with you, Abby. Every last bit."

Her throat tightened at the honesty in his voice, the truth in his dark eyes. "I love all those sides of you," she whispered. The words came easier this time, because she knew they mattered to him, even if he couldn't acknowledge them.

He searched her face, and then nodded. "Good." He bent his head to kiss her again, but as his lips touched hers, Drake shouted his name.

Jace pulled back, his brow furrowed. "You distract me from my duties," he said. "That's never happened before."

She couldn't summon up any regret. It just felt too good to matter to him, and to know that she affected him in a way no one else did. So, she shrugged. "It's not surprising. I'm kind of amazing that way."

His eyebrows shot up, and he grinned. "Humble, too."

"Jace!" Drake appeared in the doorway. "Now!"

Jace immediately turned away from her, but he caught her hand as he followed Drake into the living room, staking his claim on her in front of everyone. She couldn't help but grin as she followed him, feeling more secure than she'd ever felt in her life.

But her smile vanished when she entered the room and she saw what was waiting for them.

Chapter Seventeen

THE INJURED SHIFTER was on the couch, his torso heavily wrapped. He was pale, and his cheeks sunken, just as hers had been after Lucius's attack. His eyes were closed, and he was resting his head against the wall, as if the mere act of staying conscious was too much. His sister was perched on the couch beside him, her brows knit with concern. Kiernan was standing by the doorway that led upstairs, pacing restlessly. But it was the injured shifter that Abby couldn't take her gaze off. Such a short time ago, that had been her, almost disemboweled by Lucius.

Instinctively, she dropped Jace's hand and walked over to the couch. She crouched in front of him, her heart crying for what he'd endured, and what he'd suffered. "My name is Abby Collins," she said softly.

He didn't answer, but his sister did. "I'm Savannah Black. My brother is Roarke."

Abby looked over at Savannah. Her hair was bright red, tangled in matted knots around her shoulders.

Blood still streaked her neck, and her shirt was stained. She looked thin and worn out, as if she'd endured hell before coming to Kiernan's. "What happened?"

Savannah slipped her fingers through her brother's. "Lucius kidnapped me a few months ago. Roarke came after me." Tears filled her eyes. "He saved me."

"Lucius?" Abby asked, her voice breaking. Savannah had been held prisoner by Lucius, just like her? "Is that who attacked Roarke?"

Savannah nodded, and Abby's stomach churned. Perspiration beaded on her forehead and fear slithered down her spine like a ghoul preparing to strike—

Jace walked up behind her and set his hand on her shoulder, squeezing gently. The tight grip of fear eased at his touch, and Abby took a deep breath, grounding herself.

Roarke's eyes cracked open, and he gazed at her through slitted eyes. "Yeah. It was Lucius." His voice was rough and hoarse, as if the pain had made him scream for hours.

Nausea churned in Abby's stomach. She'd been so concerned over Jace that she hadn't taken time to find out what had happened to bring Savannah and Roarke to Kiernan's. Guilt washed over her, along with empathy so stark she could barely breathe. She stood up and pulled up her shirt, showing her stomach. "Me, too."

"Oh, God." Savannah sucked in her breath, and even Roarke made a grunt of surprise. His gaze went to her ravaged belly, and stayed there for a long time. As he stared at her stomach, his fingers tightened around his sister's, as if he could keep her safe simply by holding her hand.

"I'm so sorry," Savannah whispered, her face pale, her hand going to Abby's belly.

Abby stiffened at the touch, but to her surprise, Savannah's touch was soft and warm, somehow easing the sting of her scars. It had been amazing when Jace had accepted her body, but she'd thought he would be the only one. But Savannah didn't recoil. Instead, she was reaching out to comfort her, not afraid of being tainted by the ugliness of Abby's body.

Tears filled Abby's eyes, and she swallowed hard, trying to keep her composure.

"He said he would do that to me if I didn't do what he wanted," Savannah whispered, her eyes shining with unshed tears as she looked up at Abby. "He's a monster."

Roarke squeezed her hand. "He didn't get you." His voice was low, barely a whisper, but even so, the strength of his words was like a solid wall of steel wrapping around them all. Abby realized then that Roarke was the same as Jace, dangerous, powerful, and intensely loyal. He'd nearly died saving his sister, and she knew he'd do it again.

Jace's fingers dug into her shoulders just enough to let her know how difficult it was for his wolf to allow her to lift her shirt in front of another man, but he didn't try to stop her. Or maybe the tightening of his grip was because he knew how hard it was for her to show her damaged body to someone else, and he was supporting her. Maybe a little of both. "He doesn't get to do it to anyone again," Jace said, his voice as hard as Roarke's. "It ends now."

Roarke met his gaze, and nodded, a silent communication between the two shifters.

Drake moved closer, standing beside Savannah's side of the couch. His movement was subtle, barely noticeable, except that Abby knew he was now within reach to act if anything went south. Unlike Jace and Roarke, who emanated power and dominance, Drake was like a quiet, dangerous predator lurking in the shadows. Unnoticed, unheralded, undemanding, and yet, equally dangerous. He was understated and quiet, saying only what needed to be said, the champion who would lurk silently in the shadows until he erupted from the darkness to take down the enemy. "Savannah and Roarke saw Seth at Lucius's place."

Abby tensed at Drake's words. The blood seemed to drain from her body, and her legs gave out. She fell to her knees in front of Roarke and Savannah, her heart suddenly thundering. "Seth? You saw my nephew?"

Savannah glanced at Drake, as if looking to him for reassurance. At his nod, she turned back to Abby. "Not too long ago, Lucius brought a young boy to the same place he was holding me. He put the boy in my cell, and told me to take care of him."

Jace sat on the coffee table, his knees on either side of Abby's hips, his hands on her shoulders. "Describe the boy."

"Dark brown hair. Bright blue eyes." Savannah's face was etched with sympathy. "He never said a word to me, but I tried my best to help him. He slept on the cot with me, and I shared my food with him."

"But he was okay? He wasn't hurt?"

She shook her head. "No, he didn't seem to be, but he was so quiet. Too quiet. When Roarke came to rescue me, he tried to get the boy, but Lucius attacked him. He couldn't, I tried—" Savannah sighed. "I'm so sorry, Abby. We couldn't get him out. Roarke was barely conscious. Lucius was hunting us. I just—"

Abby nodded, blinking back tears. "It's okay. I understand." She wrapped her arms around her waist, nearly staggered by the news that Seth had been with someone kind all this time, that he'd been taken care of, that he was, as of a few days ago, okay. But now Savannah was gone, and he was alone with Lucius. A tear trickled down her cheek. "He's survived this long," she whispered. "He can make it another day, right? Until we get there?"

"Of course." Jace wrapped his arm around her, drawing her back against him. "Savannah, could you find your way back to that place?"

Abby's heart leapt at his question. Would it be that easy? Could Savannah and Roarke direct them to Seth? She leaned forward, searching Savannah's face, hope hovering in abeyance, so fragile and desperate.

Savannah paled, but she nodded. "Yes, of course."

Elation leapt through Abby. "Really? I—"

Roarke's eyes snapped open. "She's not going back." His voice was low, but unyielding, cutting ruthlessly through Abby's rush of hope. He was so angry that Abby half-expected him to rise off the couch in defense of his sister, despite the fact he was barely alive.

"No, of course not," Jace agreed easily, setting his hand on Abby's arm to steady her. "But can you *tell* us where it is?"

Savannah shook her head. "It was in the middle of the woods. I can't describe it, but I could find my way—"

"No!" Roarke struggled to sit up, sweat beading on his brow as he swayed. "Jesus, Savannah, that's how they got you last time, trying to be a hero."

"I won't let her go, Roarke." Drake interrupted.

Roarke glanced up at Drake, searching his face. After a moment, he appeared reassured, because he nodded, and slumped back to the couch. He closed his eyes, his breathing shallow and weak. Abby knew how dangerously close to the edge he was. It had taken weeks under Kiernan's care before she'd been sure she was going to live. Roarke had had only twelve hours of healing, and his injuries appeared to have been as severe as hers, if not worse.

Savannah glared at both of the shifters, then looked at Abby. *I'll go with you,* she mouthed.

"I heard that." Roarke hadn't even opened his eyes.

Savannah rolled her eyes, and Abby couldn't help but laugh in commiseration. Shifters were very difficult to outsmart, no matter how close to death they were. "I'm not going to let Seth stay there, Roarke," Savannah said. "It's not your right to decide who lives and who dies."

The affection in Savannah's voice when she spoke of Seth drew Abby's notice. During their time together, a real bond had built between Savannah and Seth. How had Lucius let that happen? Why—

Oh, no. She knew why. With a sinking feeling, she looked over her shoulder at Jace. "He was going to have Seth kill her after he'd bonded with her. Forcing Seth to kill someone who'd nurtured him would be devastating to him. He would never recover from that."

Savannah looked at her sharply. "What are you talking about? He was going to have Seth *kill* me? Never. He is a sweet boy. And he's *four.* There's no way he could kill me."

"Not until he hears my damned song." Anger rushed through Abby, chased by disgust at what she'd allowed herself to become. How had she stood back for so long and let her voice destroy so many? Just because she'd been afraid. Screw fear. *No more.* "What a bastard!" She stood up, furious. The fear of Lucius was gone, replaced by a fierce revulsion for everything he was. It ended now. *Now.* "We have to go, Jace. Seth's birthday is in thirty-six hours."

"I know." Jace held out his hand, his voice steady and calm. "We will. Come here. We still need to figure out logistics."

She knew he was right, but she was too agitated to stay still. "I can't sit." She strode away from him, toward Kiernan, who was still pacing on the far side of the room. He was tense and restless, his muscles rippling as he walked. He was still in human form, but there was a predatory nature to his movements that meant that his wolf was close to the surface. "Kiernan? Are you okay?"

He looked over at her, and she froze. His eyes had gone wolf, a haunting silver she'd never seen before. "They're close," he said.

"Who?"

"Lucius. They're hunting you. I can feel his urgency."

Abby tensed, glancing up at the ceiling. "Are they up there?"

"They never left. They're trying to get through." Kiernan's voice was low. "My safeguards will hold for now, but the threat is high. My wolf is close to the surface. I'm not sure how long I can hold it back."

Kiernan never shifted. Ever. Something had happened to him a long time ago, something horrible, and he'd never shifted since. She didn't know what it was, or what would happen if he shifted, but she knew it would be bad. "What can we do?"

He met her gaze. "They're here for you. You need to leave soon."

Her mouth dropped open. This was the shifter who had stayed up for weeks without sleep to heal her. He'd been her rock, the only lifeline that had kept her alive. To have him kicking her out was like being gut punched. "If I go out there—"

"I know. He's waiting for you," Kiernan said, regret heavy in his voice. "He's in the house. He's ready."

Jace walked up beside her. "How else can we get out of here, besides going through the house?" He sounded completely calm, as if being forced into the jaws of a waiting psychopath was an everyday occurrence. It was aggravating, but at the same time, his calmness seemed to weave a protective shield around her that enabled her to think.

Kiernan looked at him, assessing him. "There is a way," he said.

"What is it?"

Kiernan ignored him. Instead, his gaze settled on Abby. "My sweet girl," he said softly, regret in his eyes. "You have a beautiful spirit." He touched her cheek. "Your energy is a rare gift. I wish you life, not death, but your enemy is relentless. He won't let you go. I can feel the depravity of his need for you."

Jace put his arm around her, pulling her away from Kiernan. "How do we get out?" he repeated.

Kiernan dropped his hand, his gaze settling on Jace. "You're not ready. I'm not releasing you."

Abby tensed. Leave without Jace? It would be suicide. There was no way for her to defend herself against Lucius.

Jace tightened his arm around her. "I'm going."

"No." Kiernan shook his head. "The silver is still in your body. It will take several more treatments to cleanse it fully. If you were to get hit again, it would kill you. Your ankle is fragile as well. Another injury could create too much damage for me to heal."

"I don't give a shit. If Abby's leaving, so am I."

Kiernan growled low, and he turned away, bracing his hands on the wall. He took several deep breaths, his massive shoulders straining. Abby felt the strain on his control, and she realized that his wolf was reacting to Jace's show of dominance. Kiernan was definitely alpha, and yet he didn't have a pack or any social connections. He was a loner who spent his days and nights healing anyone who managed to find him.

For some reason he'd never explained to her, he resisted healing, as evidenced by the fact he hadn't gone upstairs to help them when they'd first arrived. But, if a person in need found him, he never, *ever* turned them away, no matter what the cost to himself. Just as Jace's mission in life was to protect the innocent, Kiernan's was to heal anyone who asked for help, regardless of whether they were innocent or the worst harbingers of evil, which was why he'd worked for Grigori's pack for so long. He was literally unable to turn away a request for healing. Grigori and Lucius had victimized so many that there had been no shortage of healing opportunities, until one night, several years before Abby had been attacked, Kiernan had disappeared in the dark of night. No one had heard from him again, until Abby's grandmother had tracked him down to save Abby.

She'd never revealed how she'd located him, and Kiernan had never spoken of his time with Grigori's pack, or the circumstances under which he'd finally left. He was an enigma she couldn't decipher, even after all the time she'd lived under his roof with his healing energy pouring into her.

"Leave under the light of the moon," he finally

said, his voice rough. "It's the only time that exit is accessible."

Jace glanced at his watch. "Twelve hours."

Abby closed her eyes. Twelve hours until they had to leave the safety of Kiernan's lair. Twelve hours until there would be nothing between her and Lucius except distance that would be closing quickly. Thirty-six hours until there would be no turning back for Seth. Twelve hours was too soon to face Lucius and Grigori, but it wasn't soon enough to go after Seth.

But they had no choice. The clock would continue to tick, and in twelve hours, they had to be ready. "Okay."

Jace squeezed her shoulder, then turned away and walked back to the couch. "We're leaving tonight," he announced. "Drake, build a psychic connection with Savannah to see if she can show you the way in her mind."

Savannah glanced at Drake, stiffening. "I don't want to be psychically connected with anyone. No offense, but Lucius did that to me, and I can't do that again."

Drake crouched in front of her, his hands resting lightly on the couch on either side of her knees. "I won't betray you."

His promise was simple, his words brief, but he didn't look away from her. His gaze was steady, his body strong, but non-threatening. Roarke's eyes opened slightly, and he met Drake's gaze. After a moment, Roarke nodded. "I trust him." He closed his eyes again. "He's okay."

Savannah's face was pale, and Abby's heart bled for her. She knew the fear that haunted Savannah, because she lived it too. "Drake, don't make her—"

But to her surprise, Savannah nodded. "Okay. But we do it here with everyone around."

Drake nodded. "Of course."

He held out his hand, and after a long moment, Savannah slipped her hand into his. Her blue eyes were wide as she watched Drake, but there was hope in them, hope that there really was a man worth trusting in this world full of men like Lucius.

Jace leaned over Abby's shoulder. "That's how you look at me," he whispered to her. "It's a gift no man ever forgets."

She turned to face him. "You make me feel treasured."

"You are." He hesitated, as if he were going to say something else, then he shook his head. "We need to practice the song, Abby." His voice was suddenly tense. "It's the only weapon they have that can defeat me. I need to have it under my control by the time we go out there. Is twelve hours enough?"

Her heart softened. "Jace, one minute is enough. You won't hurt me."

He pressed a kiss to her knuckle. "Don't be blind, Abby. Your love can't accomplish the impossible."

She stiffened at his words, as if the feelings were completely one-sided, as if she were some naïve schoolgirl who thought that love could change the world. "No," she said. "But yours can."

He went still. "Mine?" he echoed.

"Yes." Hurt echoed through her at the denial on his face.

Jace released her hand. "Abby," he said quietly. "Don't lie to yourself about what I am. I'm an alpha, and my duty is to my pack. I have to do whatever it takes to protect them. I've had to kill my own pack members before to protect the others. I can't do that if I cross that line and allow myself to care. My attachment has to remain distant." Regret flickered in his eyes. "Not even for you."

"Stop it." She held up her hand. "You're such a fool, Jace. Don't you understand that your ability to love is what makes you different from Grigori and Lucius? That's what makes you strong enough to fight that song. You love your pack, Drake, and even me."

"No." He caught her wrist and dragged her over to him, feral anger in his eyes. "Don't ever trust me. Do you understand?" His fingers tightened on her wrist. "*Do you understand?*" His eyes shifted to wolf, and heat poured off his body. She froze, alarmed by the sudden change in him.

"Jace—"

"Look at me, Abby. *Look at me.* I'm the man who murdered your sister. I could not stop myself. *Do not trust me.* How many men has that song turned into killers who murdered their own loved ones?"

"That's diff—"

"How many?"

She swallowed. "Hundreds." So many men who'd killed the ones they'd loved.

"I'm not different, except for the fact I'm trained to kill. I'm better at it than anyone else, and don't *ever* forget it."

His voice was so cold that chills raced down her spine. Where was the man who'd been so tender with her when they had been making love? Now, he was dominant alpha male, a deadly shifter who was pushing her away. His gaze was unflinching, so hard and cold that she stepped back. She could see the killer in him now, the dominant male who would never stand down in the face of a threat.

He nodded with satisfaction, then turned back to Kiernan, who had stopped pacing to watch the exchange. "What do you do when they pipe in the music?"

"I have a cage, and I also developed headphones that distort the song enough."

"The cage it is. I'll go in there when Abby sings to me. Where is it?"

Abby's heart sank. Jace wanted to lock himself up like a wild animal, instead of the honorable man he was? But when she saw the fierce, cold look in his eyes, she knew that's exactly what he intended.

Chapter Eighteen

JACE FORCED HIS body to stay relaxed as Kiernan's living room wall slid back to reveal a steel cage with bars so close together that even a small wolf could not get through. The steel bars were shiny, glittering at him as if they were taunting him for his weakness.

Every instinct inside him howled in protest at the idea of locking himself up. Doing so would render him unable to protect *anyone*. He would be useless, completely disempowered, which violated everything that defined him.

Kiernan handed out headphones to Drake, Roarke, and Savannah, even though no one had any evidence that Abby's song affected female shifters the same way as it did males. They didn't want to take the chance.

What if the headphones didn't work? What if Abby sang and the other shifters in the room came after her? The thought made fear grip him so strongly that for a moment, he couldn't breathe. He couldn't even conceive of being trapped in that cage, helplessly watching as the others turned on her. *Jesus*. No way. *No way* could he take that risk.

"Ready?" Kiernan said.

"No." Jace turned away. "Abby goes in the cage."

She blanched. "Me?"

"It's the only way to protect her from everyone." He swept his hand across the room. "Every one of us is a danger to her once she starts singing. What if the headphones don't work? What if they fall off? She needs to be protected from all of us."

Abby looked ashen. "I can't. You don't understand, Jace. I was trapped by Lucius. I can't—" She started to back up, away from the cage. "I can't be trapped like that. I—"

Shit. He held out his hand to stay her, his icy veneer cracking under her fear. *You make it so fucking difficult to be cold.*

She stopped, her eyes widening. "Did you just say that in my head?"

Shit. Why was he getting intimate with her? He needed to keep his distance, not bind them more tightly. Psychic communication was only for other wolves in his pack, and even then, he didn't use it much, because he didn't want to open those ties too much with the others. Keeping his distance was important for him to do his job. *No, I didn't. You're imagining things.*

Her eyebrows went up. *Liar.*

Her voice was like warm sunshine wrapping around him, and he swore. He liked it way too much. So, he glared at her, and turned his attention to Kiernan, who looked pissed.

"My headphones never fail." Kiernan's voice was cold. "She'll be safe from us." He gave a steady glare at

Jace. "It's you she must fear. Only you."

Shit. What kind of words were those? The only woman that mattered to him had to fear him. *Jesus.* He'd become a monster, the antithesis of everything he stood for. He ground his jaw, trying to keep himself focused enough to address the problem. "I don't know if the headphones work, Kiernan. I have no idea if you're reliable or not. There's no way I can trust her life to technology I can't verify."

"I'm a healer," Kiernan said. "I heal. I don't hurt. She is one of my patients, which means I would never risk harm to her." His voice had darkened, laced with the roughness of his wolf. "I work on my patients with my headphones on if the song is playing from upstairs. That is how much I trust them. *They will not fail.*"

Jace swore under his breath. What the hell was he supposed to do? Trust a stranger? He looked over at Abby, and her ashen face. Putting her in the cage wouldn't work. Leaving her with the others wouldn't work. "Fine. All the shifters go into the cage, and Abby stays outside. If the headphones work, then next time you can stay out of it, too."

"Roarke can't be moved," Kiernan said. "It's too risky."

Shit. This was such a fucking mess.

"I'm fine." Roarke didn't even open his eyes. "I want to see if these headphones work. It would be fun to fuck Lucius over by making his song useless."

Respect rushed over Jace at Roarke's response. He had a feeling Roarke was impressive as hell, and he wondered what he'd endured to get Savannah back.

Drake stood up. "I'll carry him." He bent over Roarke, and the injured shifter slid his arm over Drake's shoulder. He didn't even wince as Drake picked him up, but the depth of his pain hit Jace hard on a psychic level. Jesus. The shifter was in serious trouble. He looked over at Kiernan, reading the shifter's expression with more ease. Roarke was dying, despite Kiernan's help.

Savannah stood up, her brow furrowed. "Be careful with him, Drake."

"I am."

She followed the two shifters into the cage, but when Jace turned to go, Abby touched his arm.

"You need to be out here with me," she said. "If you know the cage is between us, you won't feel the urgency to resist."

He could tell from the expression on her face that she was serious. He didn't know how else to make her understand how dangerous he was. Yeah, she'd been right when she'd said he cared about her. He'd denied it and pushed her away to get her to use some semblance of logic when dealing with him, but it hadn't worked. He'd hurt her, but that hadn't made her any more willing to protect herself.

"I don't understand. Why can't you grasp this?" He was utterly at a loss in how to deal with her. He was accustomed to having his decisions respected and followed. He did his best to be fair and honorable, and his pack knew it. Having Abby continuously disregard his warnings made him feel like he was stumbling blind through a hailstorm, getting hammered from all directions with no way out.

She lifted her chin. "Because I know you."

"Do you?" He lightly grasped her hand and drew it to his lips. Unable to resist, he pressed a kiss to her fingertips, then ground his jaw. He touched her index finger to his incisor. "This tooth took your sister's life," he said softly. "The same teeth." Tears filled her eyes, and he felt like the biggest ass alive. "I'm so sorry, Abby. I will never forgive myself for doing it, but I would never, *ever* survive hurting you."

He released her hand and strode into the cage. He wrapped his hands around the rear bars and pressed his forehead to the cold steel as he faced the wall. He couldn't look at her. He couldn't see the look in her eyes as she recalled what a monster he was. As he heard Kieran clang the door shut behind them, he flinched. He was locked in a cage, just as he had been when he'd been in prison awaiting his trial, with nothing to think about other than the innocent life he'd just taken.

He tightened his grip on the bars, squeezing his eyes shut as he listened to Kiernan explaining proper use of the headphones to the other shifters. Back in a cell again, he was crushed by the memories, that horrific moment when the song had stopped and he'd shifted back to human, staring down at the woman in his arms. The blood. The look of horror etched on her face. The life he'd stolen.

He remembered the shock to his system, the way his body had frozen in numb horror. The scream of anguish from his soul as he prayed that he was dreaming. The cold wash of hell when he realized the blood on his hands was real, and it had been his teeth, his claws, his rage that had killed her. Never again. *Never again...*

"Put him down," Savannah said to Drake. "Let him rest."

Savannah. Jace opened his eyes in horror. A woman was in the cage with them. Yes, she was a shifter as well, but would his wolf know that? Would the song trigger only to attack an innocent human? Or would it turn him on Savannah? But he couldn't leave Savannah with Abby, in case she shifted. Son of a bitch. Jesus. What was he doing?

He spun around and pointed at Abby. "Don't sing." He ripped Drake's headphones off. "You go with Abby to help her find Seth. I'm not taking this risk. No song." He held out his hand to Drake. "Give me the gun."

"No!" Abby launched herself at the cage and grabbed the bars. "Don't you dare shoot yourself, Jace!"

Drake's eyes darkened. "You're not even going to try to defeat the song?"

Jace looked at him. "Do you have any idea of how deadly I am?"

"Yes."

"Then you don't need to ask." He was alpha for a reason: he was the toughest bastard around... impossible to stop.

"Stop it!" Abby thrust her hand through the bars and reached for Drake. "Give me the gun, Drake. Don't you dare let him kill himself. Damn you, Jace! Why can't you see beyond that stupid blood on your hands?"

"Because it's all I can see!" he shouted back. "Do you want to sing to more people? Do you? Would you sing again to a father sitting with his kids, on the chance he might not kill them?"

Her face blanched. "Don't say that—"

He strode over to the cage and grabbed the bars. "You, of anyone, know what it's like to cause the death of someone who did nothing to deserve it. What if you couldn't control your song? What if you couldn't stop yourself from singing? Would you park yourself in the middle of a crowd and just wait to trigger carnage? *Would you*?"

Wordlessly, she stared at him, then shook her head. "No," she whispered. "Never."

"Even if you're right that I wouldn't kill you, *even if you were right*, what about everyone else? Savannah? For all we know, I'd kill Seth. What about *them*?"

She gripped the bars, tears filling her eyes. "Jace—"

He wrapped his hands around hers. "I'm his weapon, Abby. As long as I'm alive, I can destroy every enemy he wants. He made me into his tool."

"You can practice—"

"So what if I learn to handle it when I'm trapped in a cell? What about when I'm in the field? Under duress? Fighting for my life or yours? There will always be a risk. I'll never be safe." He tightened his fingers on hers. "Tell me I'm wrong, Abby. Tell me that there's a way to guarantee I will never, *ever* snap."

"You could puncture your eardrums," Roarke muttered, his eyes still closed. "Pour acid in your ears. Shit like that."

Abby's eyes widened. "No—"

The faint sound of music drifted into the room, a familiar melody that was coming from upstairs. It was the song that had triggered his wolf into killing Melissa. Jace's body stiffened, and the hair on the back of his neck stood up. "Son of a bitch."

"Headphones!" Kiernan slammed his headphones on, and so did everyone else...

Except there wasn't a set for Jace.

"No!" Abby grabbed his face through the bars as the music grew louder. "Listen to me, Jace. Focus on me."

He closed his eyes, pouring all his focus onto Abby. He concentrated on the feel of her hands against his skin, on the sound of her voice, on the warmth of her breath against his cheek. But the relentless, insidious song began to get louder, whirling through the air like flames flickering in a rising storm.

"Jace!" She framed his face with her hands. "Kiss me."

He didn't hesitate. He slipped his arms through the bars and kissed her desperately. Her mouth was his respite, a soft, delicate sanctuary from the rising beast inside him. He poured himself into the kiss, breathing in her familiar scent, forcing himself to focus on the softness of her hair beneath his hands, on the taste of her mouth. But still...the song rose in intensity, beating at him with ruthless furor. His wolf paced inside him, angry, restless, hungry.

He knew he should push her away, but now that he was facing the moment, the return of the slathering beast, he clung to her, desperate to use every resource possible. It was the depth of his terror that had made him decide to use the gun on himself instead of succumbing, but now that it was here, that same terror had shifted to survival mode. He wasn't ready to die. He wasn't ready to succumb. He wasn't ready to have his life chosen for him.

I love you, Jace. Abby poured her emotions into the kiss. Warmth encircled him, cocooning him in her protective embrace, battling to protect him from the rising tension inside him.

He took her love. He accepted her kiss. He basked in her touch. He opened himself to her completely, grabbing desperately to the love she shared so freely, to the forgiveness she'd showered him with from the first moment she'd met him. He angled his head, deepening the kiss through the bars, until the song was obliterated by the raging need thundering through him. He needed Abby. His woman. His mate. His everything.

He dragged her against the bars, crushing her against the steel as he deepened the kiss, trying to get closer, to wrap her around him, to lose himself in all she was. But he couldn't get close enough. He couldn't kiss her the way he wanted. He couldn't feel her body against the length of his. Just flashes of her softness entangled with the cold, hard steel.

Frustration roared through him, a split second of anger that cracked the web of serenity she'd woven around him. The song burst through that crack, flooding him. He roared with anguish as it invaded him. His body seemed to catch on fire, heat exploding through him as hunger roared through him. He shifted so fast that he fell, crashing to the floor in a show of clumsiness unheard of for a shifter.

The moment he landed, a ravenous hunger raged over him. He leapt to his feet, focused on Abby as she backed away. He knew her, deep in his subconscious, he knew her, but it was so distant, obscured by the frenzied howl of his wolf. Bloodlust tore through him and he lunged at her. His body slammed into the bars, throwing him back. He lunged to his feet and charged her again...again slamming into the steel bars.

Pain shuddered through him, but he barely registered it. He just lunged to his feet and raced at her again. And again, slammed into the bars. His mind wasn't even functioning any more. All he could think of was Abby, of tasting her blood, of owning her...

Of killing her.

Chapter Nineteen

"JACE, NO!" ABBY screamed his name, but it was as if she didn't exist. The wolf just kept running at her, crashing into the bars with a yelp of pain, and then doing it again. His eyes were glazed, his ears pinned against his head, his teeth bared with fury. He couldn't take his gaze off her. He wasn't even aware of the others in the cell, shouting at him, trying to catch him.

He had eyes only for her.

He lusted only for her.

He wanted to kill only her.

Stunned, Abby fell to her knees, watching in horror as Jace tried to break free and kill her. He was a creature possessed, driven by a primal hunger that controlled him completely. He was a monster, just like all the others she'd created, only this time, it was so much worse, because it was *Jace*. The man she loved. The kindest, most moral man she'd ever met had been destroyed by her song.

Dear God. She was the demon, not him.

She'd thought their connection would be enough. She'd been so sure that his moral code would save him. She knew he loved her, even if he couldn't acknowledge it.

But he'd been right about the effect of the song on him, and she'd been wrong. Grievously wrong. She'd completely underestimated the sheer power of her song to obliterate any sense of the man within. After years of watching innocents succumb, she'd still held out hope that she wasn't the monster the evidence proved she was, but as she watched Jace slathering to get to her, there was no way to deny the truth.

He believed he should be dead instead of endangering the world, but the truth was, she was the one who needed to be destroyed...along with every recording of her song...which was, of course, impossible. Grigori and Lucius had replicated it so many times, there was no way to destroy them all...because she'd been too weak to fight back that very first time.

"I'm so sorry, Jace," she whispered, her voice cracking in agony. "I'm so sorry—"

The door to the upstairs suddenly crashed open. Abby leapt to her feet in horror as booted feet thundered down the stairs. "They're coming!"

Drake whirled toward the door and raised the gun, aiming at the door to the upstairs, his hand steady on the gun. "Get the key," he commanded her. "Let us out."

"But Jace—"

"Now!"

Abby raced to the coffee table where Kiernan had left the key. She ran over to the cage, but the moment she got close, Jace threw himself at the bars so hard that they bowed under his assault.

"Son of a bitch." Drake pointed the gun at Jace. "He's going to free himself!"

"No!" Abby screamed and lunged at Drake. She plunged her hands through the bar, trying to shove him off balance, but he didn't even flinch.

"I'm sorry, Jace." Then he pulled the trigger.

"Jace!" She screamed as the bullet slammed into Jace...but he didn't even slow down. He just threw himself at the cage again, bending the bars even further. She realized that the song was driving him beyond reason, beyond what his body was capable of.

"He's going to get out," Kiernan yelled.

"Jace," she screamed. "Stop it!"

He threw himself at the bars again, bending them even further. With horror, she saw him jam his head through the bars. Kiernan grabbed him and tried to haul him back, but he wrenched himself free, slipped through the bent bars, and charged her. "Jace!" She screamed again, scrambling backward as he broke through. He sprinted across the living room toward her, his teeth bared, blood staining his side.

The sound of a gunshot filled the room, and, as if in slow motion, Jace's body lurched sideways. He skidded past her, tumbling over his head as he let out a howl of agony, and then fell still in a bloody pile against the wall as Drake's second shot took him down. "Jace!" She fell to her knees beside him, sinking her fingers into his matted fur. "Please, Jace, don't do this—"

Another gunshot echoed along with shouts, but she didn't turn around. She just bent over Jace. His eyes were half-open, and he was panting heavily, his teeth bared as he watched her. She could see the torment in his eyes, and she knew the silver from the bullets was poisoning his already vulnerable body. She grabbed the scruff of his neck, and forced his head up so he was looking at her. "Don't you dare die on me, Jace Donovan. I need you. So pull yourself together, stop trying to kill me, and be the man I know you are—"

Someone grabbed her hair and jerked her backward. She clutched her hair, twisting to try to get free, but she was slammed against the floor, her face smashed into the burnished wood. Pain shot through her as fingers dug into her head, pushing her even harder into the hardwood. "If you fight me, I will disembowel him right now."

Icy cold fear gripped her as Lucius's voice scraped across her flesh. She went still, trying to think, trying to focus. She twisted her head just enough to look into the cage. All four shifters were down on the ground, unconscious, their headphones crushed in a pile of black plastic on the floor. The song, her voice, blasted through the room, like fingernails clawing across a blackboard.

One of Lucius's minions, a lean man in his twenties she didn't recognize, set a small device on the coffee table. Her voice blasted from it, singing her song over and over again. He was wearing a terrifying black helmet that apparently blocked the song somehow.

"Let's go." Lucius dragged her to her feet by her hair, then shoved her toward the stairs. Abby glanced back at the room, at the five shifters slumped on the floor. When the four in the cage awoke, they would destroy each other. Jace was dying already. Kiernan was the only one with the healing ability to save him, and he was going to wake up a shifter, and no one would be left alive in that cage.

She looked back at Jace on the floor. He was

watching her. His lips were still curled in a snarl, but his body was too weak to move. Should she stand and fight Lucius? Somehow try to save Jace? And then, what? Get killed? What about Seth? She knew Lucius was taking her to Seth. He'd want her to sing to him in person, to punish her by forcing her to destroy Seth herself. *Seth.* She had a chance to save Seth if she went, but maybe a chance to save Jace if she stayed. Or maybe they would all die no matter what choice she made. Dammit. *Jace.*

His lip raised in a snarl, but this time, instead of fear or pity for him, she felt only his torment. He was dying in midst of his worst nightmare: hurting someone who was supposed to be under his protection. She thought of how many times he'd said not to blame herself, reminding her that she'd been a child before. As she looked at Jace, dying on the floor absolutely helpless, she finally understood what he'd meant. He'd taken the blame for the murder of her sister, but she knew it wasn't his fault...just as she couldn't take the blame for what Lucius and Grigori had done with her song, or for the fact that as a young girl, she'd been unable to see a way out. She'd been a *child*, an innocent, and yet she'd spent her life condemning herself for the song she hadn't intended to create.

Lucius and Grigori were the monsters, not Jace, and...she took a deep breath...*not her*.

She hadn't been able to fight back before, but now she was different. She wasn't a little girl, and two people she cared about needed her help. Resolution rushed through her and she looked right at Jace.

His eyes followed her as Lucius shoved her towards the stairs. Jace's chest was moving in rapid, shallow breaths as he fought for air. Desperation flooded her. He was dying! "Jace!" In sudden desperately, she tore herself from Lucius's grasp and raced across the floor to Jace.

She fell to her knees beside him and grabbed his scruff, pressing her face against his. "Listen to me, Jace! I believe in you," she whispered into his ear. "When we leave, get to the table and destroy the sound box. Kiernan will heal you when he wakes up, but you *have to destroy the box*. And then come find me! I'll need you, and I love you—"

"Come on, bitch!" Lucius grabbed her and yanked her backward.

"Jace!" She screamed for him as Lucius threw her over his shoulder. "Survive, dammit, and help me!"

"Shut up!" Lucius grabbed her throat, cutting off her oxygen. Frantically, she clawed at his hand, trying to pry it off, but he was too strong. Colors spun across her vision, her lungs burned, and then darkness fell.

* * *

Fury raged through Jace as he watched Abby slump in Lucius's arm. The song still screamed in his head, inciting him to attack, but somewhere inside him, somewhere deeper, something cried out in agony as Lucius choked her. *I love you.* Her words echoed in his mind, again and again, battling with the song for supremacy. The wolf howled with hunger, rage, and bloodlust, but something else also fought to be heard. Something more primal and elemental. Something that came from a place inside him that was untainted light.

Lucius disappeared up the stairs with Abby over his shoulder, and Jace felt his soul crack in half. Desperation flooded him, and he tried to get up, tried to go to her. To kill her? To save her? He didn't know. He just had to go.

But his body didn't move.

He just lay there, inert, as Lucius raced up the stairs, taking his prey, his woman, his mate with him. Jace closed his eyes, panting desperately for air. His blood was burning as it raced through his body, searing his cells, poisoning his lungs and heart, slithering into his brain.

The song continued to scream through him, horrible, violent energy designed to incite him. The hunger continued to burn through him, but so did Abby's voice, her real voice, the voice that brought light to his soul. *Destroy the sound box.*

The sound box.

Her command rang through him, and Jace twisted his head, forcing his burning muscles to move. He saw a small black unit on the coffee table... Only yards away from him.

Destroy the box.

Urgency pounded through him as Abby's words rang in his mind. *I love you, Jace. Destroy the box. I believe in you.*

Abby. In danger. He had to get to her.

Gritting his teeth, Jace summoned his energy and with a tremendous effort, rolled onto his chest. His lungs hurt, his body screamed with pain, and his muscles seemed to be frozen. He didn't care. He just knew, *knew*, he had to stop that sound. Had to destroy the box. *I believe in you, Jace. Destroy the box.*

She loved him. She wasn't afraid. She'd come to him. He had to be there for her. He couldn't let her blame herself for his weakness. He tensed his muscles and shoved himself forward. An inch. Maybe two. But progress.

The song. The song. *The song*. It was screaming through his mind, demanding his obedience. He should be heading toward the innocents piled on the floor of the cage to kill them.

But he didn't.

He kept his gaze on the sound box and pushed himself forward again, dragging himself across the smooth, hard wood. He made it several more inches. Almost there. But so far. He fell to his side again, his chest heaving with the effort of trying to breathe. Had to keep going. Had to find strength.

He tried to move again.

Couldn't.

Come on!

Suddenly, the song didn't matter. *Fuck the song.* Abby mattered. *Abby needed him to do this.* With a roar of fury, he rolled onto his chest again. He dug his claws into the floor and inched forward again, panting as he tried. Inch by inch. So far to go. He was moving too slowly. Someone stirred in the cage. They were beginning to wake up. He was almost out of time. Had to move. One more time.

Abby. I love you. Holding the image of her face in his mind, Jace tucked his legs beneath him and sprang at the table. The black box went flying. He snatched it out of the air with his teeth, then crashed to the floor on the other side of the table.

He bit down hard. The plastic shattered beneath the force of his bite, and the song stopped. Merciful silence filled the air, and he sagged back on the floor, panting heavily, fighting for breath.

"Jace." Savannah called his name softly. He turned his head. She was on her knees, gripping the bars, her face pressed against them. The ones he'd bent had been straightened out enough to trap her inside. The others were still passed out. "I need you to get the keys to me. Abby dropped them." She pointed to a spot beside Jace's nose.

The metal key glittered, taunting him. Too far. Too fucking far. He closed his eyes. He'd done what Abby asked. There was no more...

"Jace." Savannah pressed at him relentlessly. "If Kiernan can't get out, he can't heal you. We can't help Abby. You *must* get that key to me."

Savannah's words broke through the silver-induced haze settling on Jace's mind. *Abby needed him.* With a last effort, he hurled himself at the keys. He lunged forward and swiped with his front paw, gritting his jaw against the pain streaking through his body. Victory exploded through him as his foot made contact. He batted them toward the cage as he thudded to the floor, landing directly on his bullet wound, sending excruciating pain spearing through him. He gasped in agony. And as Savannah reached for the keys, he lost the battle to stay conscious.

Chapter Twenty

ABBY WAS JERKED back to consciousness by the shooting pain in her shoulders. She opened her eyes, and then horror congealed in her stomach when she saw where she was. She was back in her old living room, chained to a hook in the ceiling with her arms above her head, barely able to reach the floor with her toes.

It was exactly how she'd awoken the last time Lucius had kidnapped her, before he'd slowly, piece by piece, begun to tear open her belly.

Every piece of furniture was the same as it had been, even though she'd moved out. Had he rented it and refurnished it to look exactly like she'd had it? Planning for the day he would reenact this? Her shoulders were screaming with pain, telling her she'd been in that position for a while. How long had she been unconscious? How long until he came back to finish it?

But as she had the thought, she noticed a family photo of her, with her mom, sister, and grandmother on the mantle. Her gaze settled on her sister, and sudden realization crashed over her. Lucius hadn't strung her up so *he* could hurt her. He'd done it so that *Seth* could kill her.

She would be the trigger that turned her nephew into the monster that had already destroyed so many lives. She didn't know how Lucius was planning to coerce her to sing, but she knew he would have a way. Who would he bring in there to torture? Her grandmother? Seth? Jace? Forcing her to make the choice between turning her nephew into a killer, or letting someone she loved suffer.

Screw him.

She wasn't going to let him win this time. She'd let him win so many other times, *but not this time.* Resolution pouring through her, she looked up at the chains binding her wrists, quickly assessing them for weakness. She tugged experimentally at them, testing their strength. The bolt was reinforced in the ceiling, and the chains were tight around her wrist. She pulled at them, using the weight of her body, until blood ran down her wrists, but they didn't budge.

Damn him!

She swung around, searching the room. The shades were drawn. She couldn't even reach the floor to stomp on it. "Help!" she screamed, even though she knew that Lucius was too smart to leave the other unit occupied. He'd thought of everything, leaving her defenseless once again.

She was out of options…unless Jace had somehow survived. She closed her eyes and reached out to him with her mind, just as she'd done when he'd spoken to her telepathically at Kiernan's. *Jace! Help! I'm at my old apartment. I need you!*

But he didn't answer.

* * *

Fear tore through Jace, a dark, penetrating fear of something horribly wrong. He jerked upright, then gasped as pain tore through him.

"Hold him down!" Kiernan shouted, and Jace swore as Drake and Savannah pushed him back down, pinning him to the cot.

Jace swore, fighting off Drake. "Let me up! Abby's in trouble!"

"He just got the second bullet out," Drake snapped. "Give him a second to get the rest of the silver out!"

"I don't have time." Jace shoved Drake away from him and rolled off the cot. He landed on his hands and knees on the wooden floor, and staggered to his feet. The room spun and he grabbed the edge of the cot to keep his balance. He was unfathomably weak, but a tremendous sense of foreboding pressed down upon him. Urgency coursed through him. He could feel Abby's fear, a deep, penetrating fear. "What time is it? What day?"

Drake shoved him back. "Sit the fuck down for five minutes."

Swearing, Jace sat down, more because his legs wouldn't hold him than because he was feeling accommodating. He closed his eyes as Kiernan set his hand on Jace's side, pouring heat into the wound. "How long do we have?"

"Not long," Drake said.

"How long is that?"

Drake ignored the question. "While you were unconscious, Savannah and I went to the place he'd held her before. Neither the boy nor Abby was there. You

205

need to track Abby."

Jace swore, and immediately opened his mind to her. He tapped into her soul, the warmth of her spirit that she'd shared with him so completely. He surrendered to her, abandoning his attempts to keep himself distant from her. He'd never forget how she'd come to him when he'd been under the influence of the song, pressing her face against his and whispering how she believed in him, even though he would have killed her if he hadn't been debilitated by the silver bullet.

She'd seen him at his worst, and yet she'd still not believed it was all he was capable of. She'd put herself directly within reach of his jaws, utterly disregarding the possibility that he might hurt her.

And he hadn't.

It would have been so easy for him to have moved his head and bitten her. She'd been so close, within range even of his depleted body, but with her fingers gripping his scruff and her words whispering to him, he'd been caught by her spell, the real spell, the spell of their connection, not the bullshit of that song. He'd been able to lie still and not hurt her, even with the song screaming in his head. It was her belief in him that had given him the strength to destroy the sound box, to battle that cursed song, and summon strength into his devastated body.

She'd accepted him completely, and now, he did the same for her, breathing in deeply the fullness of their connection. He allowed himself to think about how much she mattered to him, how she was the reason his heart still beat. He absorbed her terror, taking it as his own, reaching across the distance between them, opening his very soul to her.

He took a deep breath, opening himself still further

to her. *Abby.*

He felt her startle, and then her mind reached for his. *Jace!*

Where are you?

My old apartment. She rattled off an address, not too far from the alley where Jace had killed her sister. It was only two hours away.

I'm on my way, sweetheart. Stay alive until I get there. He broke the connection and sat up. "We're leaving now."

Kiernan scowled, but he stepped back, allowing Jace to stand. Drake was already dressed, armed with several pistols that Jace knew were loaded with silver bullets. Drake met his gaze. "Don't ever order me to shoot you again," he said, his eyes dark. "I won't fucking do it."

Jace nodded. "I won't." And he knew he spoke the truth. He'd been weak, not the alpha he'd needed to be, when he'd ordered Drake to take him down. "I take responsibility for myself."

"Good." Drake handed him a gun. "You might need this."

Jace shoved it in the waistband of his jeans. "Let's go." They turned toward the door, only to find their path blocked by Savannah. She was dressed for combat in dark pants, a dark turtleneck, and black boots. "I'm coming."

Drake stiffened beside him. "You're not."

She lifted her chin. "Seth matters to me."

"I know." Drake walked over to her. "But I got this one. You and Kiernan need to get your brother to a new location before Lucius comes back. He's still in danger."

Regret flickered through Savannah's eyes, but she

lifted her chin. "You better get Seth," she warned.

"I will." There was a moment of hesitation, and then they both stepped back. Drake turned away without another word, striding purposefully toward the stairs.

Jace glanced over his shoulder at Savannah. She was watching them go, her face a mask of yearning and fear. Jace frowned as he followed Drake up the steps. "Something happen between you two?"

"No." Drake's denial had a hard edge, telling Jace there was more to the story than he was planning to share. "Where's Abby?"

"At her apartment." He shoved the door of the closet open and stepped out into the now abandoned cabin. It stank of Lucius and other shifters, of greed and death. What had they killed while they'd been up here? Not that it mattered. They had no time. He sprinted through the cabin, jerked open the front door, and then clenched his fist in victory when he saw his SUV was still there. "Let's go. It's about two hours from here." He knew what kind of damage Lucius could inflict in two hours, and every second passing by was tearing him up.

"Two hours?" Drake swore as he yanked open the passenger door. "We'll never make it."

"What?" Jace stared at Drake as he leapt into the driver's seat, fear suddenly gripping his spine. He realized Drake had never actually told him what time or day it was. He quickly pulled out his cell phone and looked. Son of a bitch. "Seth turns five in an hour and forty-five minutes." He slammed the key into the ignition as fierce calm settled over him. "We'll make it."

Drake gripped the dash. "Damn right we will."

Jace hit the gas, and the truck tore forward, churning up the gravel. "Call Cash. We'll need backup if Grigori is there." He didn't just want Lucius. He wanted Grigori, the depraved bastard who'd masterminded all of it. Before he'd met Abby, he'd burned to stop Grigori on behalf of all the innocents he'd killed, but now it was personal.

He wanted both Grigori and Lucius to be there, and he wanted to be the one to destroy them. Not for himself. For the woman he loved.

Chapter Twenty-One

ABBY HEARD THE footsteps on the landing outside her apartment. Two sets, both heavy, both clearly men. Dear God, was Grigori with him?

She swung to face the front door as the knob turned, fighting against the fear trying to consume her. Lucius walked in first. Sleeping against his shoulder was Seth. At the sight of him, Abby choked back a cry of relief, not wanting to awaken the boy from the protection of sleep.

Then, another shadow filled the doorway. Broader shoulders, heavier muscle, eyes as dark as the pitiless hell that radiated from him. Grigori. Her father.

She swallowed as he walked into the room, walking straight toward her as Lucius walked the other way to set Seth on the couch. Grigori came to a stop in front of her, his eyes fixed on her face.

It had been so long since she'd seen him, so long since she'd stared into the eyes of the man who'd terrorized her and so many others. His eyes were shrewd and calculating, gleaming with the same intelligence that had always guided him through his massacres. "Abigail."

She lifted her chin, ignoring the pain screaming through her shoulders. "Grigori."

"You're the only one left."

"Because you killed them." She knew he was talking about her family.

"They betrayed me. These things happen." He traced a finger along her jaw, his touch so light it felt like the whisper of death before it struck. "But you're different. We need you."

She lifted her chin. "I'll never sing for you again."

"I think you will." He jerked his chin at Lucius, who strode toward the door and walked out into the hall again. "What we've discovered is that the recording of your voice doesn't have a long-term effect on the psyche the way your voice does in real life. We need you to come work for us again."

"Work for you?" She would have laughed at the idea, except for the fact that his words made chills scrape down her spine, because she knew he would have a plan. "I'm not for sale." But even as she said it, she tried frantically to process what was going on. She'd been so sure they were going to have Seth kill her. But if they weren't, then who?

"Everyone is for sale." As he spoke, Lucius walked back in the room, carrying Abby's grandmother. She was bound and gagged, her hands tied behind her back, her eyes glistening with outrage.

"Nana!" Abby gasped at the sight of her grandmother trussed up in Lucius's arms.

Her grandmother, however, just looked pissed. She

looked right at Abby and furrowed her brow, clearly commanding Abby not to give in, no matter what they did to her. "Oh, God." Abby's legs started to tremble. She couldn't let them hurt her. *She couldn't do it.*

Lucius tossed her grandmother on the couch, and Abby winced as she bounced on the old cushions. He walked over to Abby and gripped her hair, twisting her head back. "You forced me to have my wife murdered, so now you get to fill in for her. You're mine, Abby." He kissed her, a slobbery, disgusting kiss that made revulsion churn in her stomach.

"Get off!" She brought her knee up hard, slamming it into his crotch. He howled in pain, and bent over, fury spitting from his eyes as he glared at her. "There's no chance I'll ever be yours. You don't get to touch me. Ever." How long had it been since Jace had left? Two hours? Was he close? How long could she delay Lucius and Grigori?

He grabbed her around the neck and jerked her toward him. "You stupid bitch. I'll—"

"No." Grigori stayed him with one word. "Never touch her throat, Lucius, or I will cut off your hands. The rest of her body is yours, but her voice is mine. Release her."

Crazed anger glazing over his eyes, Lucius shoved her away from him. She swung on the hook like a pendulum, her shoulders now past the point of pain.

"Your nephew is going to kill your beloved grandmother. She won't be around to save you this time." Lucius grinned, his incisors lengthening. "But I'm going to make you wish that he'd killed you instead. You'll survive, just like before, but this time, you won't get away. This time, you're mine."

Anger roared through Abby. "I'm not going to sing

for you. Either of you. I'm not going to destroy Seth and my grandmother."

"You will." Grigori stepped back. "No one can withstand limitless pain, Abigail. We're going to find your limit. When you want Lucius to stop, when the pain is so unbearable you can't think, then you can start to sing. The pain will end, and you will spend the rest of your life with the knowledge that your weakness, your inability to endure, is what forced you to *choose* the path that made your own nephew turn on your own grandmother. We will break you, and you will become *mine*." Grigori pulled a chair out from the kitchen table and sat down. "And once you have enough shifter blood in you, you'll be one of us anyway. Your morals will be gone." He folded his arms over his chest, and nodded at Lucius. "Whenever you're ready."

* * *

Abby's pain hit Jace so fiercely, he recoiled violently, her pain knifing through him so intensely he couldn't breathe.

"Shit!" Drake grabbed the steering wheel, jerking the SUV back in its lane as Jace fought for breath.

"They've got her." *I'm coming, Abby. Stay with me.* Shoving aside the pain, he grabbed the wheel and jammed his foot onto the gas.

How far away are you? Her voice was weak, desperate, terrified.

Almost there.

Her anguish filled him. *Hurry.*

Fear tore through him. *Hang in there, sweetheart. You can do it.* He slammed his fist on the steering wheel and gave the vehicle even more gas. "How far away is Cash?"

"Still ten minutes."

"Shit!" Jace spun the wheel to the right. The wheels lifted off the ground as the vehicle cornered, and Drake swore as the tires screeched.

"There!" Jace pointed at the brick building three blocks away. He hit the gas pedal, hurtling down the street—

Another blast of pain from Abby had him gasping for breath, but he held tight, keeping the SUV hurtling right for the building.

Drake gripped the door. "Shit, man, you want to kill us?"

"No. Not today." Jace hit the brakes at the last minute and leapt out of the truck before it had completely stopped. He sprinted for the entrance, Drake on his heels, as he threw his shoulder against the front door, shattering the wood as he burst through. He went right for the stairs, vaulting up the steps four at a time. *I'm coming, Abby!*

He reached the fourth floor and tore down the hall. Apartment 4G was at the end of the hall, and the door was shut. He didn't slow down. He didn't hesitate. He just lowered his shoulder and charged, throwing himself against the door.

The wood splintered under the assault, and he vaulted into the room. The first thing he saw was Abby dangling from her wrists in the middle of the room, her shirt bloodied and torn. Lucius was standing in front of her, with the same half-shift he'd had when Jace had first met him.

Jace raised his gun and aimed it at Lucius, who immediately ducked behind Abby, putting her in the path of Jace's bullet. He swore and averted the gun—

Grigori tackled Jace from the side, throwing him

against the wall. Pain thudded through his injured side and he gasped for breath as Abby shouted his name. He rolled onto his side in time to see Drake crumple to the ground in the doorway. Jesus. Drake was legendary with his skills. For Grigori to have gotten the drop on both of them...*shit.*

Grigori walked over to Jace and pointed Drake's pistol at him. Jace saw in his eyes that he wasn't going to spare him. Fuck that. He had things to do, and dying wasn't one of them. He reacted instantly, lunging for Grigori. He hit Grigori in the chest at the same moment that the gun went off.

The searing pain in his chest was surreal. *Again* with the silver? What the hell? Jace landed hard on his back, writhing in pain as the silver coursed through him. His muscles spasmed, convulsing from the third hit of silver in too short of a time.

Grigori laughed softly and tossed the gun aside, turning back to Abby. "Now, he can watch. How fun for all of us."

Jace swore, rolling onto his stomach as he tried to summon strength back into his body, but his battered muscles were already drained, barely recovered from the last time. The bullet had only grazed him, but the hit of silver was already burning through him. It was the same as when he'd been shot in the cage...but the song had given him the strength to overcome the debilitating effect of the silver.

The song had made him strong.

He met Abby's gaze as Lucius turned back toward her.

Sing. He sent the command.

Her eyes widened, and he saw her glance at the couch, where the boy and her grandmother were. He calculated the distance, and he knew exactly how much time he'd have. *I got it.*

She nodded once, and then began to sing.

The shock of the words hit him hard, but it was different hearing it in person. The raw power of it was palpable, but the song didn't incite him to a rage. Abby's familiar voice poured strength and warmth into him, latching onto the depth of his emotions for her. The song flooded his body with the same fierce power as before, but this time, he merged with his wolf, keeping the sanity of the man while channeling the ferocity of the wolf. He shifted instantly, allowing the song to rip his humanity from him.

He leapt to his feet and lunged at Lucius just as the shifter was baring his teeth to sink them into Abby's torso. Jace slammed into him, crushed his throat with one well-timed bite, hurled him aside, and then spun around toward Grigori.

"Get Seth," Abby shouted. "He's already shifting! He's going to kill my grandmother!"

Drake regained consciousness and surged to his feet. He lunged at Grigori, and the alpha wolf spun to meet him. Within a split second, the two wolves were in full battle, but Drake was bigger, and he was the best fighter Jace had ever met. *You got it?*

Got it. Get the kid.

Without hesitation, Jace whirled around and sprinted across the room toward the boy. The youth's eyes snapped open, filled with fear as the song jerked him from his sleep and awakened the wolf inside him.

Jace tackled him, pinning him to the couch with his paws, meeting the boy's frightened gaze. He opened a telepathic bridge with him, pouring serenity into his mind, just as he'd done with so many young wolves so many times. Not taking time for words, he filled the boy's mind with images of wolves and shifters, educating him at lightning speed, empowering the youth to own his wolf even before the shift.

Abby stopped singing, but the youth was already shifting. His shift was quick, fueled by the song, but the moment he shifted, Jace gripped the back of Seth's neck, pinning him to the couch, holding him down as the wolf tried to take over. He held the young wolf still, keeping him from attacking Abby's grandmother, while he poured his own power into the boy to help him control his wolf.

Minutes ticked by, more and more, as Jace patiently held him still, waiting for the danger to pass. Eventually, finally, Jace felt the shudder of relief in the young wolf, the moment that the human took control back.

Jace immediately released him and crouched down, nose to nose with the youth. The young wolf was pure white with blue eyes, rare indeed. His eyes were wide as he looked at Jace, but his eyes had human intelligence and understanding. He licked Jace's muzzle, and Jace growled with satisfaction, knowing that the first stage had been successfully handled.

He cuffed the youth lightly, then turned away. Lucius lay on the floor where Jace had tossed him. Grigori and Drake were gone, but he could hear the sounds of battle from outside. He swore, racing back across the room to Abby, shifting as he ran. He caught her in his arms, lifting her wrists off the hook. She threw her still bound wrists over his neck, and he wrapped his arms around her, holding her tight. "I'm sorry I was late."

She shook her head. "He didn't do much. He hadn't

gotten started." She pulled back, her eyes glistening. "You made me sing to you."

He grinned. "I realized you're the source of my power, and it's up to me to control how I react to it." He framed her face with his hands. "I love you, Abby. That's where my power comes from. Love."

She smiled, beaming at him. "I knew you loved me."

"You were right." He slid his hand through her hair and kissed her, the first kiss of his life when he wasn't holding back. He poured everything into the kiss, everything that mattered, everything he was, and it made the kiss become more than it ever had been. "You're mine now. I'm never letting you go, sweetheart."

She pulled back, her smile fading. "I'm Seth's guardian. I'm a mom now."

"I'm in." He didn't hesitate. "I love kids."

She smiled. "You love to mold young shifters into being good, moral people, you mean."

"That, too." He rested his hands on her hips, basking in the sensation of her kiss, her commitment, her everything. "I'm yours for as long as you'll have me, Abby."

"Forever?"

He grinned. "Forever." A loud crash sounded from the hall, and he swore. "Stay here. I'll be right back." He kissed her again, and then raced for the door, shifting back to wolf form. He exploded out the door and followed the sounds of battle down the hall. *Drake! I'm on my way.*

Drake didn't answer, but Cash appeared in the doorway. "Drake's gone."

Chapter Twenty-Two

TWO DAYS LATER, Drake was still missing.

Abby perched on the arm of the worn leather couch, her hand on Jace's shoulder. Jace was beside her, once again revived after Kiernan had stripped the silver from him. Roarke was in an armchair, heavily bandaged, his face still pale. His breathing was shallow, rattling in his chest, and his cheeks were even more sunken than before. He looked weaker, as if death was tightening its grip on him, despite Kiernan's healing, but he'd insisted on being part of the discussion.

Cash and his mate, Bryn McKenzie, were sitting on the opposite couch, and Savannah was pacing restlessly. Nana had taken Seth to Jace's house, the most secure facility available, while the others had gathered at Kiernan's new location, another underground bunker he'd clearly already had in place. Jace's pack had been hunting for Drake, and no one had found even a trace of him.

Fear was pressing down upon all of them, and they were becoming increasingly afraid that Grigori had somehow taken him...except that Cash had seen Grigori and Drake fighting when he'd arrived. But by the time he'd stopped the truck and raced over to join the fight, Drake was nowhere in sight, and Grigori was on the run, disappearing into the shadows of the alleys before Cash could reach him. Cash had returned to hunt for Drake, but his scent had literally vanished outside the apartment, the trail ending so suddenly it was as if he'd ceased to exist.

"We've looked everywhere," Cash said, leaning forward and bracing his arms on his quads. His fingers were tangled with Bryn's, just as Jace was doing with Abby. "Drake's gone."

"He can't be *gone*." Abby focused on Jace tracing circles on the palm of her hand. "Grigori must have done something. He has lairs everywhere. It's just a matter of finding him."

Cash stood up. "He's my best friend. I can't sit here and wait. We have to find him."

Jace watched him steadily, his strong frame relaxed, conveying the message that he had this situation under control. Abby could feel his tension, however, in the rapid lines he was drawing on her palm. He presented complete control and confidence, but the deeply emotional and compassionate man who'd been ready to die to protect others from himself was beneath the surface, hidden from everyone except her. Jace bled silently, inside, and never showed it. But she knew, because he'd let her see it. "Abby has agreed to map out all known locations of Grigori and his pack," he said, rubbing his knuckles over the back of her hand. "We'll check them systematically. I've recalled my pack. They'll arrive tomorrow and we'll divvy up the locations. Abby and I will take some, Cash and Bryn will take a set, and—"

"I'll take a set." Savannah stopped pacing.

Roarke leveled a hard gaze at her. "You can't go in after him, Savannah—"

"I can." She walked over to her brother. "Lucius kidnapped me, but he's dead. I can handle Grigori."

"Grigori's more dangerous," Jace said quietly. "He's extremely intelligent, connected, and ruthless."

She turned toward Jace. "Which is why I'm going to help. How long do you think Drake can survive him? We all know what he's like." She looked at her brother. "Lucius caught me unaware," she said softly. "I didn't know that kind of world existed, and I wasn't prepared for it. I'm ready now. I'm not the same innocent he took. That girl doesn't exist anymore."

Anguish filled Roarke's face. "Damn it, Savannah."

"It's okay, Roarke." She walked over to him and knelt beside him, taking his hand in hers. "If you hadn't saved me, I'd be dead now. You're amazing, but now I have to pay that forward and help Drake."

Abby felt her own heart tighten. She knew what Savannah was saying. She'd also changed forever because of Grigori, seeing things she'd never be able to strip from her mind, and like Savannah, she couldn't stand back and let Grigori hurt anyone else, not if she could stop it. "We don't even know if Grigori has Drake."

"Someone has him," Cash said. "He'd be back with us if he could. If it's not Grigori, it's someone else. I'd know if he were dead. He's not."

"I agree," Jace said. "I'd know if he were dead. He's

alive, but somehow, cut off from us."

"That's why I'm helping," Savannah said. "He built a psychic bridge between us. I might be able to sense him."

"Dammit, Savannah," Roarke muttered. "You don't even know what we're dealing with." He closed his eyes. "Don't go," he said softly. "Don't go out there."

Empathy flashed across Savannah's face. "I have to, Roarke. I'm sorry. I'll be careful."

"I have an idea." Jace rubbed his palm against Abby's. "Roarke, I'll assign one of my other wolves to go with her. Tristan is an excellent fighter, and he can protect her."

"No!" Savannah shook her head. "I don't want a partner. I'm going alone."

Abby sighed as Roarke and Jace tried to argue with her. She understood Savannah. After Lucius, she had never been willing to let any man near her...until Jace. The moment she'd met Jace, she'd known she was safe with him. Somehow, Drake had done the same for Savannah, but no other male had earned her trust. Abby knew that the thought of isolating herself with another male was too much for Savannah to handle. "I'll go with you, Savannah—"

"No." Jace dragged her off the arm of the couch and onto his lap. "You're with me." He looked at Abby's face, and understanding flashed in his eyes as he read her expression. He turned to Savannah. "You can team up with us." A perfect solution that didn't require her to be alone with a male. It gave her the buffer of another woman, but the protection of a skilled fighter.

She shook her head stubbornly. "If we split into three groups, we'll cover the ground faster. Don't you understand what Grigori can do? Minutes can make a difference for Drake. Even if it's not Grigori, one minute could be the difference between life and death for him. Something's terribly wrong, and we all know it."

The room fell silent. Everyone knew she spoke the truth. Drake's life, sanity, and heaven knew what else was in danger as they sat there.

It was Jace who spoke up. "All right," he said. "Here's the situation. Anyone who gets a lead on Drake *must report it in*, and wait until the others get there. If Grigori or his wolves are around, abort." He looked hard at Savannah. "Anyone who violates this will be locked down until Drake is found. One step over the line and you're recalled from the field. Understood?"

Everyone agreed, and Savannah let out a breath of visible relief. "Okay. I agree."

Jace looked over at Roarke. "That work for you?"

Roarke grimaced. "We can't keep her here, so yeah." He looked over at Savannah. "Be careful. I'll meet up with you when I can."

She nodded. "Thanks. I appreciate that." She shoved her hands in the front pocket of her jeans. "I'm going to go catch some sleep before we go. Abby? When will you have the maps ready?"

"By morning."

"Okay. I'll see you then." Savannah pressed a kiss to Roarke's forehead, then slipped out of the room, her feet making no sound as she walked down the hall to the room she was staying in.

When she left, Jace tucked Abby more tightly against him, as if he needed to protect her the way Roarke couldn't protect Savannah. "You trust her not to go in after Drake?" Jace asked Roarke.

He was still watching the doorway his sister had disappeared through. "I don't know," he said. "She's different now. Harder. Jaded. I don't know why she's obsessed with finding him, but she is." He looked over at Jace. "She's all I have left. I can't lose her, too."

Jace nodded, his arm tightening around Abby. "I understand. We'll keep track of her—"

"No." Abby touched his arm. "You guys need to give her space. She needs to find her own power again. Lucius took that from her, and she has to be the one to find it."

Roarke's face darkened. "But if she gets in trouble—"

"Didn't you hear her? She wants to save Drake. If she gets killed, she can't save him. She'll be careful." Abby leaned her head against Jace's shoulder, suddenly exhausted. "He matters to her for some reason. She needs that."

"We all need that." Jace kissed her gently. "Let's go, sweetheart. We have a long day tomorrow."

Abby let him pull her to her feet, leaning against his side as Cash and Bryn rose. Kiernan picked up Roarke easily, and Abby's throat tightened. How badly must Roarke be hurt to have to be carried? How badly must he be hurt to let his sister leave without him? Roarke was as much an alpha as Jace, so to be left behind when his sister was in danger was against everything he lived by.

She looked at Kiernan, but he shook his head, warning her not to ask.

As Kiernan carried Roarke out, Cash walked over to Jace. He didn't say anything, but he pulled Jace into a massive bear hug. The two men held tight for a long moment before releasing. "I'd have been pissed if you'd had to die," Cash said, his voice raw. "I'm glad you're back."

"Me too." Jace took Abby's hand and pressed a kiss to her knuckles. "Thank Abby."

She started to protest, but her words faded when Cash turned toward her. "Jace matters to me," he said. "Anytime you need anything, you just let me know." He grabbed her and hugged her too. The strength of his embrace made tears fill Abby's eyes, and she hugged him back.

"Thank you," she whispered, her throat tightening. After growing up in Grigori's dysfunctional pack, she'd cherished being on her own after the attack. But the loyalty between these men was powerful, making her realize how much better life was with that kind of support.

"You're one of us now," Jace said, his gaze kind as he watched her. "You're my mate, which means you're part of the pack. You're home, sweetheart, forever."

She nodded, then her throat tightened even more when Bryn pulled her into a hug, too. "I'm glad there's another female around," she whispered. "Did you know Jace's entire pack is males? It's time to even things up a bit." She pulled back, her eyes serious. "Grigori almost destroyed Jace, and you saved him. Never forget that."

Abby nodded, unable to speak over the lump in her throat.

Jace laughed softly and wrapped his arm over her shoulder, tucking her against him. "Come on, babe. We have a lot to get done."

Abby melted against his side and waved goodnight as she let Jace escort her out of the living room to their room at the end of the hall. The moment the door was closed, Jace pulled her into his arms, kissing her with that same long, slow, delicious kiss that made her heart melt every time he did it.

She wrapped her arms around his neck and kissed him back, pouring all her love into the kiss. "I love you, Jace."

"I love you, too," he said as he slipped his arm under her legs and scooped her up, still kissing her as he carried her across the room and set her on the bed.

She propped herself up on her arms as he jerked off his shirt, showcasing the powerful muscles that still made her heart skip. "Don't we need to work on the maps?"

"We will, but first, I need you." He crawled onto the bed, moving over her like a predator about to take his prey. "I need your kiss. I need your touch. I need your love. I need it all, Abby."

Her heart softened as she slipped her arms around his neck. Her big, bad alpha, whose tenderness made her soul turn over. "I need you, too, Jace. Always and forever."

"Always and forever," he agreed, just before he kissed her, a kiss that promised the kind of love she'd never believed in, until she'd met him.

About The Author

Hailed by J.R. Ward as a "paranormal star," *New York Times* and *USA Today* bestselling author Stephanie Rowe is the author of more than forty-five novels, and she's a four-time nominee for the RITA® award, the highest award in romance fiction.

For a complete booklist, visit:
www.stephanierowe.com

Keep up with the latest Stephanie Rowe news on Facebook at www.facebook.com/StephanieRoweBooks

On Twitter at StephanieRowe2

Or by signing up for her private newsletter at:
http://stephanierowe.com/connect.php

Also by Stephanie Rowe

PARANORMAL ROMANCE

HEART OF THE SHIFTER SERIES
Dark Wolf Rising
Dark Wolf Unbound

SHADOW GUARDIAN SERIES
Leopard's Kiss (early 2016)

ORDER OF THE BLADE SERIES
Darkness Awakened
Darkness Seduced
Darkness Surrendered
Forever in Darkness
Darkness Reborn
Darkness Arisen
Darkness Unleashed
Inferno of Darkness
Darkness Possessed
Shadows of Darkness
Hunt the Darkness (2016)

NIGHTHUNTER SERIES
Not Quite Dead

ROMANTIC SUSPENSE

ALASKA HEAT SERIES
Ice
Chill
Ghost